Fire Without a Flame

by
Geneya Singleton

ISBN: 978-0-578-73381-4

Fire Without a Flame

This is a work of fiction. Names, characters, places, and incidents either are the products of the author's imagination or are used fictitiously. Any resemblance to actual persons, living or dead, businesses, companies, events, or locales is entirely coincidental.

For permission requests, please contact the author via the "Contact" page on the following website: firewithoutaflame.com.

Proudly self-published through Divine Legacy Publishing, www.divinelegacypublishing.com

Dedication

To my miracle baby Journey No'elle Singleton:

You were hand-picked by God just for me. Your life has given me the drive to live mine without any limitations or regrets and with purpose and intention. The course is set, and the world is ours.

Love, Mommy

The Charring

It was my bonding time with Dylan. I had decided to breastfeed Dylan after learning that breast milk is the best nutritional substance you could give your child naturally. I would keep the lights low, even off at times, so that we could focus on one another during her feedings. Dylan preferred a quiet environment when she nursed. Anthony's phone was just beside me on the bed. He must have forgotten it when we were packing things up for Dylan's first family outing. The tiny red notification light flashed just above the camera lens of his phone. I needed it off immediately as not to disturb

Geneya Singleton

Dylan's feeding session. I reached for the phone just in time to feel it vibrate in my hand. Fifteen missed calls!?

"Oh no!" I whispered to myself.

I hoped everything was all right. I mean, Anthony and I had so much transparency between us that we shared phones, socks, and toothbrushes sometimes. We were husband and wife and best friends.

I didn't recognize the number as any we would know. I couldn't imagine the same caller would dial the wrong number fifteen times. Maybe it was an emergency? I hoped no one had died. Anthony had lost his mother just a few years ago. Five to be exact. It was really tough for him. He was his mother's only child and a miracle baby himself. His mother had been sick most of her life. She was rather young when she died, not living to see her sixtieth birthday. We couldn't handle any bad news right now. We were still celebrating the birth of our miracle.

I decided I'd just call the number back just to calm my fears. Dylan was almost done eating now. Before I could dial the number, the "new voicemail" notification illuminated the screen. "You have fifteen new messages," I heard after dialing in to check the awaiting messages. Wow! I thought to myself this has really got to be important! I entered Anthony's passcode to begin listening.

First new message, the voice mail response system introduced. "Hey babe, where are you? I've been calling you all day. I don't care if you have a new baby. We have something special, please don't ever forget that!"

My mouth dropped open wide in total shock, confusion, and approaching anger. *Relax Ava,* I told myself. Surely this woman had dialed the wrong number and was assuming she had left this voicemail for

2

someone else, who also coincidentally had just had a baby.

I'll just skip to the next message, I thought. Dylan was done burping, so I laid her down in her bassinet just in case I had to wake my loving husband for a thorough explanation of these missed calls. *New message,* the automated voicemail assistant announced.

"Hey, babe, it's me. Please don't upset me by not answering my call. I would really hate to have to tell your wife everything! Especially how we've been involved with one another for the past nine months and how we always have unprotected sex. I don't care if you have a new baby. I need you too! Don't abandon me! I love you!"

Just as I was about to press delete because I could safely confirm that this woman had dialed the wrong telephone number, I was interrupted by the ending of her message.

"Anthony! I love you, baby! Don't leave me! I'll go crazy without you! Call me, baby! Please!"

By now my heart was racing rapidly. There was no way my husband would do this to me, to us. We didn't have any problems that I was aware of. I did my best as a wife, a lover, a friend, and now a mother. Why would this be happening? Tears were beginning to run down my face. I was enraged and beyond hurt. Anthony had fallen asleep downstairs on the sofa. I headed downstairs to address my cheating husband with my broken heart and his cell phone in hand. So many thoughts entered my mind with each step.

Before I became a mother, I was sort of a tomboy and very aggressive. My communication skills weren't the best when I was angry. I figured it was easier to allow my hands to do the talking for me. As I got closer and closer to the sofa, I could feel those retired communication skills coming back to me. *I'll ask him just once to tell me the truth and if he lies to me, I will hit him so hard, his heart will stop beating long enough for him to feel my pain*, I said to myself.

"Anthony! Anthony!" I yelled and shook his body. He was a heavy sleeper, but he needed to awaken immediately because his life depended on it. He opened his eyes wide enough to display a very confused and startled expression. He could see the tears in my eyes, and he noticed his phone in my hand.

"Oh no!" he shouted in a state of panic. "What's the matter? Where is the baby?" he asked.

"The baby is fine but apparently we are not! Please explain this number to me!" I demanded while aggressively waving his phone in front of his face as he struggled to open his eyes and fully awaken.

"What are you talking about, Ava?"

Between the deceitful tone of stupidity and confusion in his voice, my rage grew deeper. I felt my heart rate increase intensely. I could barely get a clear thought on how I was feeling at that moment. Anthony was of a lighter skin tone. Bruises would show on him like red lipstick on white paper. I was becoming lethargic. My mouth was beginning to feel like I had eaten cotton balls and glue paste. This would happen to me when I felt fully enraged, although it had been a while. I knew I could strike at any moment. Anthony was talking and probably giving a full rundown of his premeditated lies, but all I could see were his lips moving and extremely nervous hand gestures. I was already gone mentally. Tears were blurring my vision, and I was beginning to muster up enough physical strength to land a right hand, full-fisted blow to his face.

What was this betrayal about? We were best friends who had become a family. A strong unit. Didn't he know this? He had to know that this would hurt me, hurt us. Didn't he want Dylan to grow up with both parents in her life and under the same roof? Surely, he knew that something like this would tear us apart. I had a very high tolerance for pain, but this was very different. I came to long enough to hear him utter the words "I'm sorry."

"Sorry?" I repeated in my now very cloudy head. Not yet he wasn't! If all of what that bitch said in her messages had just an ounce of truth to it, he would quickly learn what it meant to be sorry. Anthony was sitting upright on the sofa now. I couldn't help but notice his hands were very close to the car keys that were sitting on the coffee table a few inches away from the sofa.

"Why are you reaching for those keys?" I asked angrily. "Are you trying to make a run for it? Did that bitch have the right number?! Are you cheating on me?!"

There was a huge lump in my throat that was causing me to trip over my words. But Anthony knew full well what I was asking, and he was surely aware of the pain I was feeling. I was naturally an emotional woman and now just a few weeks postpartum, I was an even bigger crybaby. I continued to stand before him in total shock and disbelief. Who would even want him besides me? His complexion was lighter than a glow stick in the evening sky on the fourth July; so pale and not very attractive. His smile was unusual; he resembled a Cheshire Cat. His feet smelled of moldy cheese in the summer. What kind of woman would even fathom the idea of being with a man like that? He belonged to me anyways. Hadn't he told her how crazy and psychotic and territorial his wife was? Maybe neither one of them cared or valued their lives much. It was me versus them now. I was determined to win!

Wait a minute Ava, I thought to myself. *What are you thinking about? You've just discovered your husband was being unfaithful to you and here you are plotting and planning revenge. You haven't even gotten the backstory. How do you even know what type of retaliation is necessary?* I began to regain focus. I could hear Anthony's voice again.

"I'm really sorry. Let's calm down and rationally discuss this. It's not what you think," he said.

That was it! I managed to focus long enough to catch the tail end of that bullshit request of a plea he'd made. Was he fucking serious?! He basically just admitted fault!

"How could you?!" I yelled as I plunged forward and finally released that full forced punch that I had been saving for his unfaithful, lying, cheating ass! I hated him with a passion!

"Ava! Please don't do this!" He was holding his upper lip to stop the bleeding. I didn't care If I hurt him. It was just a portion of the pain I was feeling. There was a full flow of tears running down my face. I thought I could hear the faint cries of my little Dylan coming from upstairs. The loud yelling and shouting must have awakened and startled her. Anthony had been saved by the bell. I would do anything to protect Dylan and secure her happiness. If she didn't like the loud conversations, then I would end this now but I wasn't done with him by any means.

Anthony attempted to get up from the sofa to tend to our crying daughter. "Let me get the baby while you sit down and breathe for a few minutes. I promise we will continue this conversation after Dylan is bathed and asleep for the night," he said.

I released a non-forgiving, this-is-by-no-means-over deep sigh. All I could do was rest my tear saturated face in the palm of my hands.

I had no strength to reply. Anthony rushed off to Dylan's now frustrated cries. Shortly she quieted, so I knew Anthony had embraced her. She was definitely a daddy's girl already. She would only respond to Anthony's voice during the first six months of my pregnancy. It bothered me for a while, maybe because I was a jealous mom-to-be who hadn't had the opportunity to ever establish a bond with my own father. I mean, I was her only means of survival while she was in my belly. She didn't know any better. But I felt she should have more of an attachment and responsiveness to the voice she could hear the clearest as well as being the only supplier of food and nutrition during her nine-month stay in utero. In the end, I did appreciate the bond and love she had for her daddy.

I had to go for a walk or maybe I needed a drink. I definitely needed to talk to someone about this. I didn't want to burden this alone. My best friend lived so far away, but she could calm me and keep me out of prison if anything. She was also Dylan's godmother. She had taken an oath before God to fill in for my and Anthony's absence if I took his and that bitch's life. I knew Dylan would be properly cared for.

Calm down, Ava. Take a deep breath. Your best friend is just a phone call away. Go outside, walk to the nearby park, and dial her number, I said to myself in an effort to calm my inner killer instinct. She would always answer my calls. The weather outside was warm and sunny, but somehow felt so cold. How did one really dress for the temperature of betrayal?

My anxiety grew as my ears listened for the approaching second ring to Salene. It seemed as though when you needed to vent, your feelings were a perfectly imbalanced mixture of emotions and short lived visits to reality. The sound of the ongoing ringing in my ear was so long and loud.

"Hey friend, what's up?!" Salene had finally answered. I took an additional four seconds to swallow the pain that was so unexpectedly force-fed to me a little while ago. "Hey, friend, are you there?" Salene asked. I finally mustered up the strength to respond.

"Girl!" I replied in a trembling voice. The tears were back again. Only this time I had to hide them. The park was very crowded. It was the first day of summer, so everyone was out enjoying the weather. I was a very prideful woman and couldn't stand for anyone to detect any signs of weakness within me. Not without my permission anyway.

"What's wrong?" Salene asked. "I'm very concerned. Do I need to jump in the car?!" Salene asked.

"Girl! Oh my God! Oh my God! He's cheating on me!" I bellowed out.

"What?!" Salene asked. Confusion was evident in her tone. She was notably angry for me because that's how we rode for one another as best friends for the past 25 years. "Who?! Well, not who?! But who?! Anthony?! Girl! What the hell is going on?" she shouted. I was unintentionally forcing Salene to decipher between the painful mumbling and obvious crying. She could put things together quickly. "Don't you fucking tell me that

that bastard told you he was unfaithful to you?!" she shouted.

"Girl!" I began. "He didn't have to tell me shit! We got back in from a family outing, and I was feeding Dylan. I checked his voicemail after seeing fifteen missed calls from an unknown number. There was a woman on all fifteen messages!" I said.

"What do you mean?!" Salene asked.

I'm even more frustrated now than at the beginning of our call. "Girl! He's a lying, cheating, son of a bitch!" I screamed. Now unable to hold back a single tear, I let everything freely flow through me. The pain and the tears.

"What did this woman say?!" she asked.

"She sounded really upset with Anthony and made mention of him regarding her now that the baby was here," I responded.

"What do you mean? She mentioned my God baby?" Salene questioned. "This shit is ridiculous!!" "Where is Anthony!? Where is Dylan!? No, where are you? I'm on my way! Give me a few minutes to pack a few things for the girls and we'll jump in the car!" she said.

Salene lived just a few hours away from us, but I didn't want her to come all the way here and especially with the girls. Salene had two little girls of her own, and she was recently divorced from their father. She knew this feeling and scenario all too well. I didn't want her to relive any of this. This pain was surreal, and I remember coaching her through it just a few years ago. Salene and I had a zero tolerance policy for infidelity and fuckery from any man. Especially men with whom we shared the same last name.

"No, don't come here. It's all still fresh," I begged. "I don't have all of the facts or excuses yet. I just need to vent for now," I told her.

"My heart hurts so bad for you, Ava." Salene empathized with me in a very low and understanding tone. "I'm listening, girl. Go ahead."

"This really hurts, Salene. I don't know what to do," I said. "How did you handle the beginning phase of the shock?" I asked emotionally.

"The same way," Salene said. "I wanted to die, girl, but not before I killed him and his whore," she added.

"That's exactly how I feel!" I expressed.

"You can't let him break you this way. The pain you feel is valid, but you've also just had the baby, so everything is going to feel amplified," she said. "Get your feelings out, but don't give that bastard the satisfaction of taking advantage of your vulnerability and risk more conversations about you over his pillow talk with his mistress."

Salene was right today, as she always was when it came to giving sound advice. She got through her messy marital issues and divorce gracefully. I don't know anything about being graceful with anyone who could cause me such pain and misery. He needed to feel every ounce of pain that he had inflicted upon me.

"Ava, listen to me. This is very important, so I need you to hear me clearly." Salene helped me refocus my attention back to her.

"I'm here, girl, go ahead. I am listening to you," I stated. "Anything is going to help at this point."

"I want you to remember that Dylan is your beautiful baby girl. She is your miracle baby. Recall how long and hard Anthony and you prayed for her to become a part of both of your lives. She needs you more than anything right now. Any irrational thoughts you're having about this situation, as bad as it pains you, cannot, I repeat cannot, be acted upon today or tomorrow. Your and Dylan's lives are depending on your response to this situation. I know you want to kill them, but you may end up doing something that could change life for you for the worst. Promise me you will sit and talk with Anthony and see if you can get to the bottom of things?"

"Okay, girl. I promise," I regretfully committed.

"You know I'm here if you need me?"

"Yes, Salene. I know you are. Thanks, girl," I said as I wrapped up my much needed girl talk. "I'm walking back to the house now to check on the baby. He's already called me three times since we've been on the phone."

"Please call me before you all go to bed or if anything goes south," begged Salene. "We're going to get through this together," she said.

"I promise," I said. She was always there for me no matter what she had going on in her life. I was getting closer to the house and could feel the anxiety setting back in. Many of the overwhelming emotions were hitting me again. I was a little more focused to a point of holding a civilized conversation with Anthony. Maybe he was afraid of how I would continue to react because I found him sitting on the sofa with a gauze pad in his mouth. He was asleep again; this time with Dylan fast asleep on his chest. He was probably using our baby as a shield of protection and I must admit, he made a good decision because I certainly had some more frustrations to release.

His phone was sitting on the coffee table where the car keys were before I had left to get some fresh air. The keys were gone. I was sure Anthony hid the keys because he knew I would have packed up and Dylan gone and stayed somewhere for a few days. I hated to deal with things before I was ready to confront them. I dealt with problems in my own timing whenever we were faced with any conflict. I would leave or walk away until I felt emotionally competent enough to address the issue at hand. That might not have been the ideal approach to certain types of marital issues, but it was best for me and my previous anger problems.

It was almost evening. I was pretty tired from our family outing earlier and had been looking forward to a nice shower and a full night's rest. Dylan was beginning to sleep through the night now. Most newborns don't give their parents that kind of peace until they are at least six months of age, especially breastfed babies. I became lost in my thoughts for a second as I mentally reviewed our marriage. We had what I considered regular marital issues. I mean, mostly any couple could get past financial and intimacy issues. Hell, I even looked past his sweaty feet and their constant battle with fungus. They carried an odor of aged cheese, and I was the one who had to do the laundry. I worked hard to get past these small issues because I knew we would have bigger fish to fry. His struggles with ambition would become warning signs that I intentionally ignored later in our marriage. I chose Anthony because he was a hard catch when we were in high school. He was very popular among our peers. His unmatched wit and charm made all the girls crazy about him. The competition was high, but I was a girl who was always determined to get what she wanted and I would fight for it by any means necessary. He had been dating one of the most beautiful, but very arrogant, girls in our class. Her name was Amore' Lyman. She'd already hated the very air that I breathed, so I figured why not fuel her fire even more. I pulled out all stops available to eventually steal Anthony from her and live happily ever after . . . or so I thought we would.

The feeling that I was being watch pulled me out of my memories, and I looked up to see Anthony staring in my direction with what appeared to be a combination of remorse and uncertainty. I wished he would just keep his eyes focused on the baby or hell, even the empty bottle of water that I had asked him to throw out earlier that day. For a former military professional, he certainly was not the cleanest man. That water bottle had actually been on the coffee table for two days now. Come to think of it, he never really participated in any of the household chores. I did the laundry, the cooking, and most of the cleaning. It was me who sorted out our monthly bills each payday. It was me who did the grocery shopping and kept the shopping list up to date. He would help out with Dylan as much as I would allow him to. Maybe I did miss a few red flags, but who wants that perfect love anyway? Anthony was his mother's only child while I was one of eight children. I was raised by a single mother who had shown me how to maintain a household. Well, excuse me for being so mature and responsible.

I hadn't had much time to get to the nail salon every other week like I did before Dylan was born. Certainly, there was no time to make hair appointments. Dylan was still so young. Although I would never doubt his love and pure efforts, he would put forth in caring for Dylan, Anthony just wasn't "mommy." He could change diapers, make bottles, and maybe even brush her hair but he also thought it was fun to toss her in the air like a rag doll at times. He didn't realize that she was too young for that kind of play.

Geneya Singleton

I was contemplating using the same hand he asked for in marriage to leave a reminder across his high yellow face. Oh, how quickly had he forgotten the crazy black woman that resided in me. He deserved so much to come face-to-face with the back side of my hand, but the baby was resting peacefully in his arms. My blood was at a boiling point, but I was listening. I was ready to hear the many bullshit excuses of why Anthony thought it wise to go out and cheat on me.

"Ava," he said.

All of a sudden, the very way my name fell from his lying tongue made me want to change   my identity. He could have my first name as a packaged deal with his sorry ass last name when I divorced him and ran away with Dylan as far as that joint bank account that only I know the balance of would carry us. This pain pierced me more than the eighteen hours of labor I had endured with Dylan. Dylan, oh my precious baby. How would the divorce that I was painfully contemplating affect her? I thought I had finally put an end to the vicious cycle of children being born out of wedlock in my family. For the first time in several generations past, a family was created where we all shared the same last name. I never wanted to become a statistic like many women I knew. I wanted so much more for Dylan. She deserved to be raised in a household with both of her parents. Maybe Anthony hadn't thought his actions through or the associated consequences, but he was about to learn the hard way.

I had gotten so lost in thought, that I'd forgotten he was about to explain the location of his penis since it hadn't been in his pants our entire marriage.

"Ava!" Anthony shouted as he had taken notice of my blatant disregard for his presence and conversation.

Fire Without a Flame

There go those lying lips moving again, I thought to myself.

"I know you're angry with me," he said. "I can explain this whole thing. It's not what you think."

As the tears began to fall down my puffy cheeks again, Anthony stared in my direction with a look of total remorse. I knew he hated to see me cry. He hated even more so to be the cause of my tears.

"She's not...we're not sleeping together. She's a friend of my cousin Trevor." Still utilizing my available patience, which grew thinner by the second, I continued to listen. "She's an older woman and she's crazy in the head, so she has been playing around on my phone prank calling."

I gently removed Dylan from his arms. She was still asleep. I gave Anthony the impression that I needed to embrace my precious baby to console my broken heart, so he was not suspicious of my sudden reach for her. I removed our daughter from the chest that housed one of the coldest hearts I've ever known and laid her down in the bassinet we had set up in the next room. I closed the door quietly behind me so that she would not hear what was about to take place

If that bastard thought for one second that he was about to insult my intelligence the way he had just done with that lame explanation, he was definitely mistaken. I couldn't get back to him fast enough with his awaiting reminder I had in the form of a clenched fist. I returned to find him with his head down in the palm of his hands, probably planning a continuation of that bogus story he just tried to feed to me. I was getting closer to him now with my dominant hand in position. Still looking down, Anthony began to spew out more lies like venom from a poisonous snake.

"I'm sorry, babe. Now what were you saying?" I asked, to distract him from my steadily rising fist.

"Look, Ava, let's just have dinner and act like this never happened."

Before he could finish his thought, I felt a gust of wind sweep between my fist and his lying face.

"Ava! I know you're upset with me but hitting me will not fix this! Did you forget that our baby is in the next room?" he asked while rubbing what I hoped was a broken jaw.

"Where were your concerns for 'our' baby when you were out playing house with that bitch?!" I yelled in extreme anger.

Anthony stared at me with tears filling his eyes. They were a light hazel color. It was the one of the things that had attracted me to him years ago. Mine were a deep brown, and together we had given Dylan the most beautiful shade of grey. At this moment I was beginning to hate every physical aspect of his being. I wanted Dylan's features, even her full DNA makeup, to completely change. I wanted her to have nothing in common with this bastard that was sitting before me. The stream of pain that he had caused so suddenly stung like a hive of bees against my heart. He began to speak again. This time I was too weak to interrupt.

"I know I hurt you. I hurt us, but I will fix this. You are my wife. We are a family, and I will do whatever is necessary to make this right. I will get rid of her; she means nothing to me. I will call our Pastor and arrange some counseling sessions," he promised.

I continued to listen even in the midst of the excruciating pain I was in. Betrayal was ever so present. My husband was now my enemy, and if an enemy presented himself to me, he must be prepared to die before me. Anthony knew me well. He should have realized that my heart would break into a million pieces. We had prayed so long for this family that we'd created together. My wrath was greater than God's at times in my eyes. My heart was big enough to love the world, and if you were lucky enough for me to share it with you and you betrayed me you would pay greatly. I could hear his voice faintly in the background. I was too busy plotting my revenge to listen. Why he thought he could do something like this to our family and then dust off his Bible and set up marriage counseling sessions with our pastor was beyond me. Anthony would remember that he had crossed me, and he would never make this same mistake again.

I began to mentally scroll the names and numbers in my little black book that I had kept tucked away for a rainy day. I thought that I'd retired that book to never open again, but my intended actions would be justified during this storm. Wait, what the hell was I thinking? Who would want me? I was just a few weeks postpartum. I couldn't fit anything past joggers and yoga pants. I still had a belly that resembled a pregnant woman during her first trimester. Honestly, if I couldn't lay eyes on Dylan myself every day, I would think she was still in utero.

Who cares! I thought.

I would wear the hell out of a jogging suit and a sexy pair of pumps. A little red lipstick and a quick call to my hair stylist, and I would be ready for revenge. One of the many things about my personality that men adored was my unique sex appeal and uncontested charm. I could talk the pension payments out of a sugar daddy. Anyone whose path that I had ever crossed over the years, especially with my former line-up of men that I snagged during one of mine and Anthony's mini break-up sessions when we were younger, maintained a certain level of love, trust, and loyalty. I could call any one of them up today and we would pick up exactly wherever we'd left off, no matter how long it had been. I could use a change in scenery anyway. I was always home with the baby while Anthony worked, and I was already tired of the monotony of being a housewife; cleaning the house and changing diapers day after day. I needed to get my groove back, and there was no better time than the present. If Anthony did not see the value in me enough to remain faithful, he would experience every karmic retribution that was due to him.

I thought I could hear him speaking again. I had zoned out long enough that I was sure he had to be aware that I was no longer listening or giving a damn about what was being said.

"Ava. Ava, are you here with me baby?" he asked.

"Okay, Anthony, do what you need to do," I replied. *Because I'm going to do what I need to do*, I added silently in my head.

I continued on in deep thought. Who from my past could I reach out to that I would have immediate access to? Derron! Derron was one of the best lovers I'd had. I'd call him first on my list. He was definitely a blast, and I knew that he would greatly appreciate hearing from me. We'd shared the most extreme chemistry. We never had a need to speak many words in the bedroom. We knew exactly what we wanted and needed from one another and connected in the most beautiful way. Who else could I call? I began running through my list again in my mind. Anthony was still speaking. I could care less. At this point, he could drop dead and I wouldn't budge. Dylan would always know who her father was, but I would have a new "daddy" really soon. The thought alone produced mixed emotions. Derron certainly spoke my language in the bedroom but it was love that we could never find between us. Casual sex was fun at times, but love made it all worth it. I never followed the masses. I was a woman of my own caliber. Love over lust.

"Ava! Ava! Talk to me baby!"

Ugh! There was that annoying voice again. Anthony knew me well. I'm sure he could see the plot of revenge forming in my brown eyes. I had never cheated before. The thought had never crossed my mind, but anyone who had the balls to cross me would remember not to do it again.

"Yes, Anthony? I'm sure you see me sitting here. Why do you keep calling my goddamn name? I heard you loud and clear. Give me my space damnit!" I shouted. "How would you process all of this if I had brought this shit to you so casually? Seriously! Get away from me!"

I walked into the next room to check on my poor Dylan. She could probably hear the breaking of this marriage in her sleep. She was still resting so peacefully.

I could sure use a tall glass of wine right about now, I thought to myself. I just wanted a way out from this mind numbing pain. As long as Anthony kept his distance from me for the rest of the day, I would be able to contain my rage.

Maybe I wouldn't wait until we were divorced. I mean, Anthony sure did just whatever the hell he wanted to do in this marriage. I was sure he would never agree to an amicable divorce anyway. He was very possessive and jealous. He knew exactly what I brought to the table. The very thought of me being with anyone besides him would give him chest pains beyond a heart attack, which didn't sound like such a bad idea at that moment.

He was definitely worth more to me dead than he was alive. His life insurance was paid in full. Maybe I could just add a little special ingredient to his dinner tonight? Dylan was still very young; she would forget about her father in no time. By the time she needed a male figure in her life, I would be happily married again.

Oh, who was I kidding? I couldn't hurt anyone. I just wished I could make him feel a portion of the pain I had in my heart at that moment. He claimed to understand my feelings, but I knew he really didn't. I was in complete shock and total disbelief. I knew I hadn't always spoken to Anthony in a way that a wife should speak to her husband if she loved and respected him, but he hadn't always made things that simple. He spent most of his adulthood being as carefree as a boy in his teenage years. He needed redirecting so often. I just figured it was a woman's job to help create structure and to keep the foundation of the relationship strong. I guess I was wrong. Maybe his whore made his sense of irresponsibility and immaturity a thing he could be proud of?

Honestly, I really didn't give a shit! If he wasn't happy with me, he could have left a long time ago! I felt that I was too old to start over, but I damn sure wouldn't stay in this mess of a marriage just to save face. I was very private when it came to my personal affairs. The rumors and added speculation would just buzz around between both of our families and friends. So many people had not been rooting for us from the beginning, and now the day had come. The day that they had all prayed for. We hadn't made it as a couple. A failed marriage. The idea made me cringe. Would I have to put that on some sort of social resume? What kind of man would want a woman who couldn't even hold on to her marriage for more than five years? We failed miserably. No! Wait! He failed! He failed us! I played my role as a wife, and I played it very well. He was the one who wanted to hold public auditions.

Forget this shit! I thought. I was leaving all of this behind me, and I would be exiting this marriage with the self-dignity and pride that I walked into it with. I would tell my version and he could tell his!

"Ava,

the baby is asleep. She has her mouth wide open just like you do when you're asleep." He was speaking to me again.

"Listen Anthony, you can save your small talk and weak ass attempts at a peace treaty," I said.

"I am going to take a nice hot bath, with a very tall glass of wine. You can listen out for the baby and stay the fuck out of my way until I have a stable enough conscience to participate in any form of dialogue with you."

As I walked off into the kitchen to grab my favorite wine glass, I could feel the hairs on the back of my neck stand tall. I knew Anthony was staring at me with that pitiful look on his yellow, now noticeably dry face.

"Get some moisturizer or something, motherfucker," I mumbled under my breath. He had a lifelong battle with eczema just below his chin and down to his neck. *Maybe his little whore should have been taking care of his skin condition just the same way she was taking care of his penis,* I thought to myself.

Geneya Singleton

"Ava, I love you more than life. You and Dylan are my world. I was nothing until I found you and I am going to do whatever it takes to keep you if you will have me."

By the time I had walked back from the kitchen, I was close enough to him to hear the tail end of that bullshit statement. With my favorite glass and half full bottle of cabernet in hand, I headed up the stairs to start my bath. He just as well could have been talking to himself because I sure was not listening.

Between the steam coming from the bath I had drawn, the soft jazz playing in the background, and the sweet aroma of sandalwood from my favorite candle, I almost felt like I was in another place. A peaceful, warm jacuzzi situated just outside of a cabin in the mountains was where I had placed myself. Just God, me, and nature. I slowly closed my eyes and sank down as low as I could into the lavender scented water. Gentle pecks of bursting bubbles felt like soft tickles from nature against my now shimmering skin. I'd intended to take small savory sips of my wine but when I picked up my glass, I noticed that there were just a few drops left. I must've gulped it down like the first sip of water after a Saharan desert tour. I glanced over at the bathroom sink, remembering I had brought my bottle of wine upstairs with me, so refills were in reach. Just as I replenished my well-deserved glass, I could hear footsteps coming toward the bathroom door.

"Ava, I just wanted to check in on you," Anthony whispered between the cracks of the 'do not disturb me, you cheating bastard' securely locked bathroom door.

I couldn't have pressed the volume button hard enough on my wireless speaker to drown out his annoying voice. I knew that Dylan wouldn't be disturbed

22

by the suddenly elevated music because she had slept so peacefully through many arguments between us before.

I guess he'd gotten the hint that I was not in the mood for more conversation because I could hear his uninvited footsteps departing from the door. I readjusted the volume and returned to my place of solace.

My bath water was beginning to reach room temperature. I preferred the water to be very hot, almost to a boiling point. The water felt like little waves that dispersed warm hugs all around my body each time I moved. I could sit in the water for hours at a time. It was my safe haven whenever the world would consume me with obligations. I would also run to a bubble bath whenever I'd felt overwhelmed by the baby. I didn't require much for peace in my home or in my mind. I started thinking to myself again.

Anthony's mistress probably made life feel like a walk in the park for him.

What kind of responsibilities could he possibly share with her?

They didn't have any financial obligations between one another, or did they? Since their relationship was such a secret, what else could Anthony be hiding from me? I wondered. Could he have children with this woman? Maybe they shared more than a fling here and there. What if Anthony had fully betrayed me and had given this woman a baby? What kind of woman would be so foolish and so desperate as to fall in love with a married man and even more, one who was expecting a baby with his wife? As psychotic as I had imagined her to be, maybe she hadn't known about me initially, but at this point I really didn't care. My mind wouldn't stop working overtime to answer the questions I was developing in my heart.

What was I thinking? I might never get a full or even a true answer from my cheating husband. They could not have possibly spent as much time together as she was claiming because Anthony and I were pretty much joined at the hip for most of our relationship and marriage.

I could hear him setting the dinner table as if he thought that I would dare to even sit down and share a meal with him. I could smell the scent of my favorite dish baking in the oven. It was the heavy, warm smell of melted cheese and tomato sauce. Mozzarella, to be exact. The sauce must have dripped down onto the oven just above the broiler because a perfect aroma of slightly fire-roasted sauce and bubbling cheese emitted in the air. I knew it was Anthony's famous lasagna. He would always make this dish for me when he had been fucking up. The delicious bribery would definitely win me over in the past, but this time he could take every carefully laid piece of pasta and choke on it! At least this kind of death would definitely be an accident and I would not have to go through any interrogations.

I finished the bottle of wine, and my bath water was a little cold now. There was no need for slipping into anything sexy after my bath, so I found an old pair of Christmas-themed pajamas, applied a mud mask to my face, and climbed into bed to sulk and plot for the rest of the evening. About an hour had gone by and I was still lying in bed drowning in tears and buried in thought. After Dylan was asleep for the night, maybe I would give this mistress a call so I could get her side of the story. I wasn't sure if I really wanted to know the extended version, honestly. I felt like I had no more tears left in me to cry. I also could not be certain that my temper wouldn't have me track her down like a fugitive on the run and put a whooping to her. Suddenly I could hear the joyous sounds of cooing coming down the hall. Anthony was on his way into our bedroom with my beautiful Dylan. I could feel the happiness in her voice as they approached me. She was always so excited to be with her daddy. I couldn't fathom the idea of taking that away from her, but I was sure once she was old enough to understand why I had to make certain decisions for her and I, she would respect me for it.

"Are you going to join Dylan and me for dinner?" Anthony asked.

I just reached my hands out for my baby girl and ignored his attempt for conversation. Anthony left Dylan and I for some much needed bonding time. I was sure if Dylan could speak, she would tell me to lay off all of the kisses. I smothered her with lots of them whenever we were together. The warm smell of breast milk and baby wash all over her just made me cling to her like a magnet. I showered her with lots of love and affection. She would never feel as empty as I did in life, especially today. We played and laid together until we had both fallen asleep.

Embers

Dylan must have been as exhausted as I was because the sun was in full bloom the next morning when we woke up. She hadn't awakened even once for a feeding. I looked over to the other side of the bed and noticed that Anthony hadn't slept with us the night before. Hopefully he'd gotten the message loud and clear that his presence was not welcomed in our bedroom, or even our lives anymore. Maybe he'd tiptoed out to be with his mistress while we slept.

I headed downstairs to confirm things and found him fast asleep on the sofa with our wedding album open on his chest. I guess his guilt had carried him on a one-way trip down memory lane. I hoped he enjoyed his visit there because he would never see a day like our wedding day again for as long as we both shall live. He awakened from his sleep and immediately jumped up from the sofa as if he were startled or maybe even terrified that I had been hiding a murder weapon behind my back or underneath Dylan, who was resting in my arms.

"Good morning, my beautiful ladies," he said as if either of us were going to respond.

I handed Dylan over to him and headed for the kitchen to make a fresh cup of coffee for myself and to prepare a bottle for Dylan. I was in no condition to be able to produce enough breast milk for her. I was too exhausted mentally and emotionally. I kept a few prepared bags of formula in the freezer for emergency purposes such as this. I sat at the kitchen table and enjoyed my freshly brewed coffee while Dylan's breakfast was warming in a cup of hot water. I could hear Anthony in the next room talking to her. He was telling her how he had hurt mommy's feelings really bad and was going to fix it by any means necessary. I was sure she knew he was full of it just the same as me, but at least he cared enough for her to express some form of remorse even though she couldn't understand a word of it. I finished my coffee and finished preparing her bottle. I handed the formula off to Anthony and gave Dylan a kiss on the forehead as I headed back upstairs to my room. This time I would not be there to sulk and cry all day, I was going to sort through my pre-maternity clothing to see what could still fit me. I planned to get out of the house today and enjoy some much needed mommy time. Today we wouldn't discuss a word about yesterday. Today I was going to feel alive and free. I was not going to be a mother or a wife. I was going to be me.

It took just about a half an hour to get to the bottom of my closet where I kept most of my sexy apparel. I'd found my favorite pair of distressed jeans with a cute "off the shoulder" top. Both fit very comfortably as I tried them on and practiced a few minutes of "cat walking" in the mirror. A smile appeared across my face unexpectedly. I was so silly when I wanted to be. I entertained myself naturally, as a loner typically has the ability to do. I rambled through my drawer of accessories to find the cutest earrings and necklace to go with my outfit. Once I found a nice pair of shoes to match, it was definitely over for these Christmas pajamas and Anthony for at least today. I made a call to my hairstylist and scheduled an appointment for later that morning. I realized I would need a friend or two to hang out with tonight. No sense in going out solo when you looked as good as I was about to within the next few hours. I made a few calls to some old girlfriends and we confirmed plans to play catch up later that evening at a local lounge.

I was really starting to come out of my funk and slight depression. I hadn't mentioned a word of my plans to Anthony. He would learn of things as I was walking out of the front door. Almost the same way he had done to me the night before. I packed a small bag for my evening attire, took a quick shower, and slid on a comfortable jogging suit and tennis shoes. I made my way down the stairs to head out for my hair appointment. The look on Anthony's face was priceless. He didn't know if I was moving out or just moving on, and I didn't speak a word to him. I stopped by his seat on the sofa to give Dylan a big kiss and then gracefully made my exit. He knew not to say anything to me, especially while the swelling was still present on his face from yesterday's news report. He'd awakened the beast in me, and I was on a roll. I walked my fed up ass right out of that front door and slammed it so hard I think I heard a few screws hit the floor. No need for Anthony to repair it since he obviously enjoyed residing in broken homes.

It felt good to get out of the house even if it was under unfortunate circumstances. I inhaled a full breath of the outside world then jumped in my car to get the day started. I arrived at my hair appointment and was warmly greeted by Raymond, my stylist.

"Ava! It's been so long!" he shouted.

We exchanged the warmest hug. It was definitely appreciated since I was hurting so bad inside. I preferred male stylists because, to me, men were honest about their opinions, especially when it came to women and hair. Raymond would always style me in a way that was appealing to myself and men since my very first appointment with him over ten years ago. We chatted about the hot topics in our lives and our families. Raymond was like a big brother to me. He had always provided me with sound advice and direction, but I was too embarrassed to share with him what was going on between Anthony and me. The salon was too crowded that day, and I didn't want to risk anyone overhearing our conversation.

Although I refrained from sharing the details with Raymond, he could tell that there was something unsettling about my energy. He didn't pry or harass me for details but instead promised to make me look and feel like a million bucks when he was finished working his magic hands. Raymond definitely kept his promise because when he was finished with my hair, he spun me around in his chair to admire it in the huge mirror hanging from the wall by his station. I couldn't believe my own eyes. I had truly gone through a transformation. My hair felt so silky and soft. The tightly wound curls bounced around in free motion just like you would see on those shampoo commercials. I couldn't thank Raymond enough. I felt like a new woman. The soccer mom look had gone away and MILF had taken over. I paid my bill and headed off to my next stop. Anthony had called my cell phone once while I was out of the house, and I forwarded it to voicemail. I didn't need any negative energy around me while I was restoring my mind. I was sure if it was an emergency with Dylan he would have called again or even texted. I couldn't worry myself with those kinds of thoughts right now. I was getting back to finding myself today and nothing or no one would stop me.

The next stop on my list was the massage parlor. Nothing relieved emotional pain more than the strong hands of a kind gentleman providing me with a rub down. I knew just the place to go. It was a parlor that I had frequented before my pregnancy. My favorite masseuse there was a fine tall gentleman by the name of Christopher. He was young, strong, and very easy on the eyes. Deep tissue massages were his specialty. One hour of a rub down from Christopher and I could probably postpone my revenge on Anthony.

Twenty minutes into my massage I could feel much of the tension leaving my body. Every muscle in my body felt much more relaxed, and I was beginning to feel rejuvenated. If only a happy ending weren't illegal here, I would've certainly added it to my package. Speaking of which, I could see Christopher's staring right at me while I lay on my stomach facing his abdominal area. My hormones were running rampant. It wasn't my fault; they had been imbalanced since I had given birth.

Oh, stifle yourself, Ava! I chastised myself quietly. This is not the way to go. I wasn't a hundred percent sure that I would leave Anthony for good, so I didn't want to do anything irrational, at least not yet anyway. No sense in both of us jeopardizing the marriage.

After my session ended, I decided I would change into my evening apparel right in the restroom. I could just go out for a drink or two alone. Although I had made plans to meet up with a few of the girls, I honestly wasn't ready to face anyone while all of this was going on in my marriage. If I had had one too many drinks, I would probably become a little loose and end up sharing much more of my life than I should with a group of girls that I wouldn't see but once a year. I decided to go for it and started out into the city for afternoon drinks and a much needed solo date with myself. After three glasses of chardonnay and a delicious Cobb salad accompanied by some old school music that filled the lobby of the sports lounge, I was floating high on life. I danced with a guy that appeared to have been out on a solo date as well. We laughed and joked and enjoyed a very stimulating conversation. I was having a ball. I glanced down at my phone and noticed the time. It was close to 5 p.m. I had better head home and check in on my sweet Dylan. I said my goodbyes to my newfound friend and went on my way. I was glad that I had decided to pamper myself and implement a few good methods of self-care. I thought I was ready to listen to Anthony and his explanation of infidelity. I arrived home and entered.

Anthony must've been upstairs with Dylan because the lights were out downstairs. I dropped my keys and made my way up to see my baby girl. I missed her so much whenever we were apart for more than a few hours. As I walked up the stairs, I could hear Anthony speaking. I figured he had been talking to Dylan again about his marital screw up, but as I got closer to the top of the stairs I could hear the conversation more clearly. Anthony was actually on a telephone call. The plush carpet that covered the stairs must have insulated the sounds of my arrival because he didn't seem to realize that I was in the house.

"I told her you were a friend of my cousin's. She is upset but she doesn't know much about us. I'm confident I can persuade her into believing me. I will go through a few sessions of that stupid marriage counseling just to make my sincerity more believable. I can't have her leave me just yet. I need more time with my daughter. She is still so young. After a few more months I will tell her the truth about us, and you and I will be together forever. I love you and our unborn child more than anything. I don't want to be here with her anymore. You already know this. The past few years with you have been amazing. I just need you to be a little more patient with me baby. I will leave her, and you and I will continue to raise Dylan and our son together. I need you to stay focused on the light at the end of the tunnel. Amore', I have never failed you before and I will not start now. We will live the life that we missed out on in high school. I believe you and I were destined to be, and I am sorry that I allowed Ava to get into the way of that. I am coming home, baby. Please trust me on this."

A bright light shining in my eyes was the first thing I saw when I awakened.

"Ava, hello, Ava, can you hear me clearly?" There was a man standing over top of me. He wore a white lab coat and had a stethoscope draped around his neck.

"Where am I?" I asked as I attempted to sit up on the strange bed.

"Ma'am, you are in the hospital's emergency department," the guy with the lab coat said.

"Emergency department?" I asked. "What's going on?" I began to tremble, and dizziness fell upon me.

"Ava, try to relax a little. You were brought in by ambulance. Apparently, you fainted and would not regain consciousness, so you were rushed in."

Tears began to fill my eyes as I remembered the last thing that had occurred. I recalled standing in the hallway of our bedroom and overhearing Anthony on the telephone professing his love to his former high school girlfriend, Amore'. Maybe it was all a dream and that's why I was here.

"Where is my husband? Where is my baby?!" I shouted in a panic. I was afraid and completely confused.

"Please calm down, ma'am, before you faint again," the doctor warned me. "We will go and get your husband and sister for you now."

My sister? I thought to myself.

Anthony hadn't cared much for any of my siblings, so I couldn't imagine which of them he had reached out to rush to be by my side. I saw the curtain that led to my bed draw back. I could identify Anthony's wedding band from a mile away. For the first time in the past few days, I was happy to see my husband's face. As he drew the curtain back further, I could see an additional shadow following closely behind him. I knew it had to be Sophie. We were the closest of my mother's children. She had to be devastated to learn of what had happened to me. I blinked for an extended period of time as I attempted to regain stability from the aftereffects of fainting and whatever medications the doctors had administered to me. The second I reopened them, I could see Anthony approaching me and a woman followed behind. I couldn't be sure if the medication was causing me to see things that weren't really there. It was her and she was holding my sweet Dylan in her arms. Her belly was protruding, and it was obvious that she was pregnant. The conversation that I had heard between Anthony and her was, in fact, real. Anthony was cheating on me with the very woman that I had stolen him from years ago. This couldn't be real. He had the audacity to bring her here and she was holding my daughter. She stared at me with a sly smirk spread across her now aged face. I could see the shadow of revenge all over it.

"You son of a bitch!" I shouted at Anthony.

"How could you do this to me?!"

"Ava, you need to calm down. You had to have seen this coming. I'm sorry you had to find out this way but come on! You know the rules of the game. How you get them is how you lose them," he told me.

There weren't any tears left in me to cry. I wanted to be sedated so badly. Anthony had thrown a dagger right through my soul. "Hand over my baby, you crazy bitch!" I shouted at Amore'. She just smiled as if she found humor in all of this.

"You may have her for now, but Anthony and I will be filing for custody of her along with his decree of divorce," she threatened. I attempted to leap from the hospital bed to snatch Dylan from her arms and to beat the skin off of her.

"Have a seat, Ava!" Anthony shouted. "It's over. You never respected me as the man of our household or in this marriage. I got so sick and tired of pretending to be happy with you," he said. I began to scream in anger. My increased heart rate had triggered the monitors and suddenly my room was swarmed by all kinds of hospital staff and two police officers.

"What's going on here?" one doctor asked.

"My husband and his fucking mistress over there are threatening me and holding my baby hostage."

"Ma'am, you need to calm down!" one officer said. By now my Dylan was crying her poor little heart out.

"Will everyone stop telling me to calm down!" I shouted.

"We will sedate you if you are not able to settle down on your own, ma'am," a doctor said.

"I am the victim here!" I shouted. "Why is everyone attacking me?!"

The officer came close to my bed and whispered. "Ma'am, your husband is pressing charges against you. He said you hit him in the face while you were drunk and belligerent, and he doesn't think your baby will be safe with you. The doctors have confirmed alcohol in your system and the bruise on his face is evident. Please cooperate and we can have this go as smoothly as possible," he said.

I am in no position to win this, I thought to myself. I had to dig deep to find a way to get through this ultimate level of betrayal that would keep me out of prison and to get Dylan back in my arms.

"I understand, officer," I said. I was now calm and willing to follow the instructions of the officers and physicians present in my room. I had to do this for my daughter. "May I have a word with my husband alone?"

I asked the officer. He looked over to Anthony to confirm his approval of my request. Anthony nodded and the officers and hospital staff began to leave the room. "She needs to give me our daughter and get the hell out of here as well," I said to Anthony. Amore' handed Dylan to Anthony and left the room. I burst into tears once again, in total shock and disbelief.

"Why are you doing this to me?" I asked him.

"I hate the very air you breathe. I've been planning to leave you for quite some time now. I held on for as long as I could. You just don't do it for me anymore," he admitted.

I was speechless. Who was this man that was speaking to me this way? How could he be so hurtful after all we'd been through together?

"I will drop the charges under a few conditions," he said.

"I want half of your retirement savings. You can keep the house and the car. We will split visits with Dylan between the two houses. We can agree amongst ourselves to these requests, outside of a courtroom. I basically am asking for an uncontested divorce. I want to make this as quick and painless as possible for the both of us. I am moving on with my life and you will do the same. Do you agree before I call the officers back in this room?"

"I agree," I said with streams of tears falling from my eyes.

"Good. I will give you a few minutes with Dylan alone," he said. With that, Anthony left the room. I cried and hugged Dylan tightly. I promised her that I would take care of us, and that I was sorry this was happening to us. I know she didn't understand a word of it, but I

Geneya Singleton

needed to assure myself that I would follow through with
any promises that I'd make to her.

The Spark

Two Years Later

It was right before the onset of fall, and they hadn't fixed the air-conditioning the correct way in the car. For the second time that week, I was back at the mechanic's. What time was it? The daycare was closing soon. Thankfully, it was walking distance from that godforsaken shop. I'd just stop past and drop this car off for them to take advantage of my single, independent ass again. But, hell! Who else was going to help me? I entered into the small business and was greeted by two men who appeared to be non-productive and surprised to see another sign of life present. The business didn't seem to have many customers to service. One was an older man, about sixty years old. The other was a young man, maybe thirty years old.

"Hello, I was here a few days ago for an issue with my car. My air conditioning unit had not been working properly, and I had it serviced here. You guys said there was a possible shortage in the wiring or something like that," I said with the most sarcastic 'you know you didn't fix it correctly the first time' tone of voice I could find.

"Oh yes! Let's pull up your file so we can take another look at what's going on," the older guy said.

"What's your name again, ma'am?" the other, younger guy asked. This guy, he was oh so fine, fair brown complexion, with dimples and a chiseled chin. He had face that said, 'I'll take your first born and one kidney and you will wrap them both in a red bow and be happy about it.' He was wearing a navy blue uniform with an "Emergency Response Team Paramedic" logo stitched on the front right pocket of his shirt. Certainly, this was not his field of expertise.

"Did someone call 911? Why are you here? And why are you asking my name? Actually, why are you in my business?" I asked.

"Wait just one minute, sweetheart! Take it easy! I work here. I just left my full-time job, and I work part-time here. I didn't mean any harm. I'm just trying to help locate your paperwork. You seem to be in a hurry. Anything I can do to expedite that, I'm obliged to do," he said.

At that point my heart rate became elevated. A smile hid ten feet behind my pride. My legs weakened so I decided to have a seat. There was something about the way he spoke.

Stay focused, Ava! You know you should not trust men so just cross your legs, fuck that smile, and forget his charm. Besides, the daycare is closing soon. You don't have time for good guys and laughs. You're a single mother with a broken air conditioning unit in your car which, by the way, you have a payment due for soon. Ugh, snap out of it! Tell him to mind his business and leave with the same low esteem you walked in here with, I thought to myself.

"I'm sorry, gentlemen my name is Ava Hampton. Now, can whomever is responsible for my paperwork gather it so I can get this car on a lift and go on about my way?"

The older guy, Stan according to his name tag, agreed with a sly smirk on his face. "Yes, ma'am. It's my responsibility to follow up with this. Let me just shuffle through this pile of paperwork and we'll have everything we need to get started and get you going."

"Yes, please do that!" I replied in an annoyed, sarcastic voice.

The paramedic was staring me down trying to force a smile as if he could control my facial muscles and I stared back. I felt an unusual sense of energy coming from him. It was heavy, like we had known each other before. He had a smile that could pierce your soul, but I was not in the mood for that although deep down inside I didn't want this, whatever it was, to end.

Keep a hard look. Maybe he will think you're another evil bitch with an unnecessary attitude and actually mind his business as requested, I told myself. I had been in this trance for so long, I'd almost forgotten the shop owner was still fumbling through his unorganized pile of paperwork trying to locate my file.

"It's in here somewhere, ma'am. I'll keep looking." With a smirk on his face, he had taken the opportunity to add his two cents to mine and that fine paramedic's moment. "Oh, she might be a little soft on you, Marcus," he told the paramedic.

So that's his name, I thought to myself. Well, he didn't look like a Marcus. More like a soul-snatching Derek. Marcus added to the awkward moment by conceitedly agreeing and now exposing the full depth of those dimples on each side of his face.

"Yeah, Mr. Stan, I think you're right," Marcus replied.

They both proceeded in stupid macho guy laughter. I mean, it was kind of nice to have that kind of attention after the day I'd had. We were short staffed at the bank again and it was the beginning of the month, the time where retirees and disabled persons received their monthly government payments.

I didn't think I'd even had lunch that day.

Snap out of it, Ava! I told myself. *It's too soon after your divorce to even think about dating and besides, the daycare will be closing soon.*

"I hate to break up this little party, gentlemen, but I need to run to pick up my daughter before her daycare closes...unless one of you will be accommodating my one dollar-a-minute late fee?" I asked sarcastically. I was just looking to make my exit before Marcus decided to whip those dimples out again, and I asked him to marry me.

"Oh well, you can just leave your car here and get to your precious bundle of joy and I promise to have everything situated once you return," Stan said.

"Okay, Stan, I'll be back in twenty minutes," I stated with a detectable undertone of a threat and a promise.

"We'll be here when you get back. Please don't keep us waiting too long." This time it was Marcus who spoke, and those dimples were in full exposure. Also, in full view were my weakening knees.

I wondered if I could get up from my chair and make a graceful exit without anyone noticing the obvious butt pads I had foolishly decided to try out today of all days. Most men seemed to have this unavoidable desire to look at a woman's ass before they'd even notice anything else about her. I mean, it wasn't my fault, or his, that God had given me more breasts than he did ass. Well at least today I had more to stare at.

I'd heard that the padding could appear deflated after sitting for long periods of time, and not in unison. Well, I couldn't worry about that now. I was certain I looked pretty silly still sitting after I'd announced my departure more than five minutes ago.

Well, here goes nothing, I thought to myself as I mustered up the courage to get up from my seat.

It was the moment of truth. I quickly leaped from my chair and ran for the door. I could hear a deep masculine moan coming from Marcus' direction as I made my exit out of the front door. I wondered if that was a moan of intrigue or if it was more of a grunt of disappointment. A slight moment of panic began to creep in. Were the buttpads lopsided or uneven? Small beads of sweat were forming around my lip-stache. I was too nervous to look back into Marcus' direction. I may have ruined everything. He appeared to be the type of guy to fall for very pretty, sophisticated, and confident girls. Because of my poor decision making in attire for the day, I may have just let a man with great benefits get away. He would be back to looking for other girls with real booties in no time.

I walked as fast as I could out of that door and never looked back. I figured if it was meant to be, he would be there when I returned just as he had promised.

The weather was perfect that day. The sun was shining, and the wind felt like a gentle whisper across my face as I walked to get to Dylan. I was always anxious to get to my baby girl after work. She was just a little over a year old. This age had appeared to me as one of the most fun and innocent milestones of her life. She was getting better with her communication skills, and we were almost to a point where we weren't on a first name basis. Dylan was a little parakeet. She would hear others call me by my first name so she figured it had to be the one she would use besides "mommy."

She was learning and growing at a rapid pace. I just wished her father would be more consistent in her life. He was missing out on so much, especially the shared responsibilities of parenting. If I had to call out from work one more time because Dylan was sick, I would be unemployed again. I had lost my job during my pregnancy because of company mergers and consolidations. The changes hadn't made life completely challenging for us. Back then the sperm donor, I mean my husband, had been there to financially support us while I stayed home preparing for the arrival of our daughter. After I had given birth to Dylan, I was afforded the most wonderful opportunity to be a stay at home mom. Anthony worked full time and had a pretty good job with great benefits, and we could pay all of our bills on time. The merger at my old job had taken place towards the last trimester of my pregnancy, so I hadn't been out of work long before my current job had given me a call.

I was getting closer to the daycare center; I could tell from the laughter coming from just a few feet ahead of me. They must've had the windows slightly cracked to let some of the fresh air and gentle breeze enter the classrooms. Dylan was such a vibrant little person. She was the most good that had come from that awful marriage. She laughed at everything I would say; she was my reason for living. Motherhood was my biggest dream since childhood.

I would be the best mommy to Dylan. After all, I was playing a dual role. I had to be mommy and daddy. Not having my father in my life and still battling that experience, or lack of, in my thirties made me want to ensure that Dylan would never feel that kind of pain.

"Hey, Dylan's mommy!" The little people shouted in unison. It's so adorable how the children would learn which parent belonged to each child at such a young age.

"Mommy!" There was my baby girl, running to me with opened arms!

"Hello, my baby! I shouted, "Did you have a good day?!"

"Yes," Dylan replied in her tiny voice.

"Good, let's get your things on and take a little walk to our car."

"Car?" my little parrot repeated.

"Yes, car, Mom-mom," I replied.

Geneya Singleton

Our walk would take a few minutes longer than it should. We were just a few blocks away from the auto body shop, but Dylan's little feet and curious mind would have us stop at every freshly bloomed flower and mysterious animal walking along. While Dylan babbled on in toddler talk, I was able to steal a moment of mommy thinking time. Was he still there waiting for me as he had promised?

Oh, snap out of it girl! He's got you blushing inside already and just from a small but flirtatious hello. But he is fine as hell and I do mean fine, I mused to myself.

"Mommy! Mommy!" Dylan shouted.

My private moment was over.

"Yes, Dylan?"

"You see a cat?" she said excitedly.

"Yes, baby. Mommy sees the cat," I replied, although it appeared to be on its last life… I mean, they did get nine, right?

We lived in a moderate income neighborhood. It was a sort of tradition to abandon your pets onto the streets after they were no longer cute and cuddly. It was sad, honestly.

Rumor had it, the local Asian restaurants would take the strays in and cook them up with the daily prepared meats. I don't know how true it was, but I would stick to the fried chicken and rice dish whenever I patronized the restaurants. I mean, the chicken appeared to be chicken. I hoped it was anyway. We were just a few more minutes away from the auto body shop.

Play it cool, girl. If he likes you, he will show it, I told myself. I couldn't help that my palms were beginning to sweat a little as I was kindly informed by my outspoken two-year old after I firmly grabbed her tiny hand to head across the very busy street.

"Mommy, your hand is wet." Dylan said.

"Sorry baby, mommy forgot to dry her hands from the water," I said. Anything to take her mind off of it, especially before she decided to say something embarrassing in front of her new stepfather.

I giggled to myself at the thought. I mean, I was no fast mover to love, but I did have intuition beyond most human abilities. I knew a sure thing when I saw it. I also had always gotten whatever I wanted, whenever I wanted it and Marcus was certainly something I wanted.

Okay, focus now, I thought to myself as I slowly opened the door to the shop. "Careful, Dylan", I instructed my little princess as we approached the front door of the shop.

The outdoor steps were in poor condition. The cement was cracking and by the way they'd "repaired" the air conditioning unit in my car and how they maintained their filing system, I could bet my second born that they weren't going to repair the steps anytime soon or have the financial abilities to pay out if my baby tripped and fell on their property. It was safe to say that I had a zero tolerance policy when it comes to anything or anyone trying to cause any direct or indirect harm to my child.

"You sure kept me waiting long, I was beginning to worry about you," Marcus said when we entered to waiting area.

I had already learned the deep tone of his voice within that short period of time that our souls had connected. I didn't even need to look up. I gave my bruised heart permission to muster up just enough positivity to communicate with my brain to let my mouth know it was okay to smile a little. No need to confirm for the charming prince that he had touched something within me, although I'd let him touch more if this worked out.

"I'm sorry, I didn't know you'd still be here when I got back," I stated as if I wasn't dying to see him again.

"When I give my word, I stand by it sweetheart," he said.

For some reason I wanted to smile much harder than my face would allow. Keep your cool, girl. You look funny when you smile wide. He'll think you're a little special or weak for him and we can't have that, not so soon anyways. "I like that," I said to Marcus. "It's admirable." We exchanged smiles long enough to make full eye contact. It could've been me, but I could feel something strong coming from Marcus. My curiosity wouldn't allow me to leave it alone. I just need for him to ask for my phone number so we can get this thing moving.

"Mommy, I want paper and crayon."

"Say please, Dylan."

"Please, mommy," she replied.

"She's so adorable," Marcus complimented.

"Thank you," I replied.

"How old is she?"

"She just turned two a few months ago. She's such a character," I added.

"No need to make mention of that, I have a three year old myself. My boy can be quite the character as well. He keeps me on my toes. And I'm a first time dad, so I'm learning as I go."

"Sure," I agreed. "Children can be so much fun to raise and be around, but they'll sure find a way to give you a run for your money. Especially at this age," I said.

"Yes, definitely," Marcus agreed.

Now I needed to know a few things of importance. Where was this little boy's mother? What was the nature of her and Marcus' relationship? I'd heard all about how some co-parenting arrangements can be. One day the parents were still fooling around together and the next day they were just two people who happened to share the same child. I didn't need any more drama in my life.

The short conversation between Marcus and me was so intriguing. We talked about parenting and the struggles of co-parenting. A small part of me would escape with each word that was spoken. I could feel myself slowly letting down my guard. Time didn't exist while I was in his presence. Dylan was coloring so peacefully sitting next to me that I had almost forgotten she was in the same room. She must've felt the calming vibrations that Marcus somehow brought into the room just like I did.

It felt as though we'd known each other for years. We shared an unusual form of chemistry. We had made direct eye contact during the entire conversation. His soul spoke to mine and I could hear every word that flowed from it. It must've been at least an hour of this soul exchange. I knew I could not allow Marcus to leave me without getting his contact information. Just as I felt the urge to ask him for his phone number, Stan burst back into the waiting area where Marcus, Dylan, and I had been sitting.

Geneya Singleton

"Well, I think I have found the problem!" Stan shouted as if he had had an epiphany. "It appears that your air conditioning motor blower is completely shot."

That was the last thing I needed to hear. The only thing I could think about was the phone call I would make to the finance company, letting them know that this month's payment would be late yet again. My credit scores mimicked that of a young adult with no established credit history: deplorable.

After Anthony and I split up, finances were scarce. He, of course, did not have the slightest bit of concern for my ability to survive beyond our divorce. I tried my best to live within my means, but basic living expenses had gotten the best of me. The house had been in foreclosure three times in the past year and the car payment, with its balloon interest rate, hadn't made things better. The judge that granted us our divorce had suggested that we sell the house so that we could both possibly walk away from this messy marriage with a few coins.

Unfortunately, we owed more on the house than it was worth, so it just made more sense for Dylan and I to remain in our home for the duration of the loan term. That time equated to a little over ten years. I figured by then, Dylan would be much older and more able to adapt to change. I had planned for us to move to Texas once the timing was right, and we would start our new life there. I felt Texans were more friendly, given their natural southern hospitalities, and the career opportunities were endless. I would never feel the guilt of moving my princess so far from her sperm donor because I knew he really wouldn't give a damn, much less fight for her.

Fire Without a Flame

Anthony wouldn't stay from under his unhealthy, low self-esteemed whore of a girlfriend long enough to probably even notice Dylan and I were thousands of miles away. I had it all mapped out. Dylan would be starting her fifth year of school in a friendly and peaceful neighborhood and I would find the job of my dreams and get my business ideas off of the pages of my diary.

"Are you still with me?" I could recognize that deep, sexy tone in a crowded room by now. Marcus must have noticed my mental drifting. I did that so often. I loved to have conversations with myself every chance I could get. I was so used to being a full-time mommy, that every available time slot, mental and physical, pretty much belonged to Dylan. I was an overthinker, so having these often life changing conversations alone was priceless. I came to just enough to acknowledge Marcus' request for my returned attention. Somehow, I could tell that he was demanding it and not asking for it.

"Yes sir. I am definitely still here with you," I responded.

If Marcus thought he was the only one who could be flirtatious and seductive, he was oh so wrong and I would remind him as much as I could. Stan was awaiting a response from me as well. I could see him in his filthy uniform standing beside his unorganized desk. I had to acknowledge my soon-to-be husband first. Stan could wait, just as he'd made me wait when I arrived earlier.

"If you were still with me, then you would know that I see something in you that is making my mind focus solely on you in this moment. It's quite distracting, but I like it. Also, Mr. Stan is needing a response from you about how to proceed with taking care of your air conditioning problem," Marcus told me.

Geneya Singleton

I couldn't quite put my finger on this feeling that ran through my body each time Marcus made a request or demand for me to do something but whatever it was, I felt a strong urge to acknowledge and respond to it.

"My apologies, Stan," I stated with a feigned expression of concern. "What are our next steps and my available options to have this problem resolved with my vehicle?"

"Are you able to leave your car with me for a few days?" Before I could respond with the burrowing sarcasm that I had been building up for Stan, Marcus interjected.

"I'm pretty sure this young lady probably needs her vehicle to transport her precious cargo around and to get to work. That will probably be a huge inconvenience for her," Marcus observed.

"That is correct," I responded, and we spent the next few minutes hashing out the details to get my car repaired. When we were finished, Marcus seemed to have an important thought in the moment that prevented him from parting ways with me at that moment.

"We've been spending all of this pleasurable time together, and I have yet to get your number."

It was then I realized Marcus was not only very attractive, but also smooth in his flirtatious abilities. We had both gotten so lost in this ongoing exchange of energy that I would be remised if I had not given him my contact information.

"I'm pretty sure you can find that in the same file that Mr. Stan here, has spent much of his precious time locating," I replied with every ounce of intentional sarcasm measurable.

"I will certainly take you up on that suggestion," Marcus said. "It was a pleasure in meeting you and your beautiful daughter," he added.

"Oh, believe me, the pleasure was all mine," I replied while attempting to return the flirtation and mental seduction. Marcus reached over to my seat and gently grabbed my hand. He cupped it into his and with the lowest, most deep tone in his voice said, "You couldn't begin to imagine how the pleasure of meeting you has been most favorable on my behalf."

If it were physically possible, I felt a warm sensation beginning to fill my once cold heart. I could feel the emptiness that I had carried for so long begin to leave my soul like a spirit transitioning into another dimension. Marcus could read me like he was the sole author of my life story, and I was ready for him to flip through every page. Stan remained standing with a sly grin on his face, curiously staring at Marcus and myself. His eyes raced back and forth between Marcus' and mine. He knew that a match had been made between us. I knew it as well.

Oxidation

E ach morning started with a strict routine. I would awaken Dylan with her favorite nursery rhyme of "Twinkle, Twinkle, Little Star." She would slowly open her eyes and display the most innocent smile.

"Good morning, beautiful," I would say in a very low voice.

"Morning, beautiful," she would repeat back to me.

"Let's get ready for the day," I would say.

"Okay Mommy!" she'd reply.

Geneya Singleton

My mornings with Dylan were fully loaded and would vary from day to day. I never had time for coffee or even breakfast some days. I focused all of my attention on my baby girl. After breakfast, a playful bubble bath, and a short chase around the house to get her clothes on, we would head out the door while the morning air was crisp and the sky mirrored soft blue puffs with a dusty tint of orange like randomly ignited flames as the sun began to appear from behind the clouds. Today the morning air felt brisk, so I had to strap Dylan into her car seat quickly and tune into her favorite animated show on her tablet and cover her little legs with her favorite blanket. I listened to breaking news headlines on the radio and waited for the car to warm up.

My phone would typically never ring during my morning routine unless it was a coworker informing me of their late arrival. Anyone who knew me personally knew how much I hated to be distracted by frivolous conversations while I prepared for the day. Suddenly, there was an incoming call. This time it seemed that the phone rang with more of a loud tone than usual. I didn't recognize the number. Maybe it was him. Maybe it was Marcus. At least I hoped it was. It couldn't be. I didn't think I would hear from him so soon and so early in the morning, but I was really excited nonetheless if it were. The incoming call rang again as I was attempting to gather my thoughts and clear my morning voice before I answered.

I also didn't want to pick up right away, so as not to let him in on my anticipation. My phone was connected to my car via Bluetooth, so I snuck a glance in my rearview mirror to ensure that Dylan was still preoccupied by her cartoons. I didn't want her to get the sudden desire to hold a conversation while I spoke with her soon-to-be stepfather because she too, would be able to hear his handsome voice.

"Hello?" I answered in the softest voice I could find within.

"Good morning, beautiful," I heard through the surround sound of the speakers in the car. His voice was so deep and alive as if he had had his morning bowl of happiness.

"Who am I speaking with?" I asked in an intentional tone of surprise and confusion.

"This is your dream come true. Marcus," he responded in his familiar voice of seduction and confidence. I took a quiet deep breath before responding.

"Oh. Good morning dream-come-true. It is such a pleasure to hear from you." As if I had not been thinking of him all night.

"Well, I'm sorry to call so early in the morning, but I work an overnight shift and it just ended and you were on my mind, so I had to reach out to you. Is this a good time to talk?"

"For you, of course," I said. "I'm heading to take my daughter to her daycare before starting my own work shift. She's preoccupied so we can chat. How was work?" I asked.

"Work was pretty quiet. One small fire set by some mischievous kids to some shrubbery nearby."

"Oh no!" I shouted.

"Don't worry," Marcus replied. "We were able to put it out quickly and return to the fire station, so I was able to sleep peacefully for the rest of the evening."

"Wait a fire?" I asked, as I had just remembered that his uniform from the previous day had identified him as a paramedic. "I thought you were a paramedic?" I asked to catch him in his first lie.

"Oh, I am," Marcus responded. "In my station, we wear both hats. Every firefighter is also a trained paramedic. I am a firefighter first, and if and when we are short staffed, I cover the ambulance or paramedic's division."

I was even more impressed by him. I could tell he was bold and brave and spontaneous, but this occupational discovery just confirmed it. He was definitely a keeper so far. Dylan must've felt the peaceful vibrations coming through the car speakers from Marcus' voice because I could see her smiling warmly in my rearview mirror.

"So, tell me something about yourself that would make me want to call you again," Marcus requested in a very flirtatious voice. I knew he would be expecting a very bold and most likely kinky response from me, so I decided to give him just the opposite.

"You are calling me more than likely before you have even brushed your teeth," I said. "That would make me one of the first thoughts on your mind as soon as you opened your eyes this morning. I'm pretty confident you will have a need to dial this number again."

There was a slight moment of silence. Dylan let out a sly giggle while I awaited a response from Marcus. I glanced in my mirror to see if she had picked up on her mommy's sarcastic confidence only to find her face deep in her tablet. She must've been laughing at something she was watching. I returned my attention to the present silence.

"Did I lose you?" I asked with a smirk on my face.

"I'm sorry, I'm still here." Marcus replied.

"Barely." I said. "I hope I didn't say anything wrong?" I asked with a fraudulent tone of concern.

Marcus let out a short but deep breath and said, "I think I like you."

"I know," I replied. Before he could add anything else to my rebuttal, I realized that I had arrived at the daycare. I had gotten so lost in the ambience of our brief conversation, that I hadn't noticed I'd driven so quickly. "I hate to interrupt this lovely conversation, but I've just arrived at my first destination. Can I call you back in a few minutes?" Before he could respond I added, "I would also like for you to take this time to reflect on your available options."

"And what options would that be?" Marcus asked.

"I would like for you to consider the fact that I have made it into your head and that I am coming for your heart shortly. I would also advise you to proceed with caution."

There was another moment of silence, then Marcus responded, "I can appreciate the warning, and I opt to stick around to see what is in store for us. I would also offer a word of advice."

"I'm listening," I replied.

"I was born under the moon of the zodiac sign of a Taurus." I began to scratch my head with a dazed look of confusion while I awaited an explanation. "When I speak, there is always an assumed period at the end. I will particularly lead in all cases, and I have every intention of taking control of your mind, in a good way. Shortly thereafter, your heart will follow so I thank you in advance. You will most likely forget about every man you've ever known before me, including your father, because I know he was not around much to begin with. My advice to you would be to open your mind and allow the rhythm of your heart to flow on purpose and enjoy what's already been awaiting you. Lastly, before you call me back, please be ensured that I will never mislead you and will always respect you. But understand, there will never be another to cross your path like me."

At this point I was pretty confident that my heart had skipped a few beats if it hadn't stopped beating altogether. I maintained the moment of silence trying to gather a bold, but sarcastic response. This time I did not have one. Marcus' statement had touched me in the most unique way. Our friendship was in the premature phase, and I had felt for a moment that he may have been moving faster than I would like, but it was something about the way he'd spoken to me that made me somewhat comfortable with it. As a single woman, I had been calling the shots for so long, I may have just loved the idea of someone else directing my thoughts for the moment.

Finally, I mustered up enough strength in my tongue muscle to respond, as if one was needed or even allowed.

"I understand."

I played it back in my head in that same second. *I understand? Is that all you could come back with, Ava? He probably thinks you're strange now. Oh well,* I thought to myself. My words were out in the atmosphere, no going back now.

"Good girl," Marcus replied. "Now take care of your little girl and call me back when you can."

"Oh, I will," I replied.

The volume in the car's speakers had been loud enough for me to hear the sudden disconnection of our call. I had to sit for a few minutes before getting Dylan out of her car seat to go inside of the daycare. I was an over-thinker naturally, but this time I really needed to process what had just happened. What did he mean when he called me a "good girl"? Oddly enough, it didn't feel disrespectful or juvenile. It actually sent a tingle through my spine. I wasn't sure what I was in for with this guy, but I knew I already liked it.

"Let's go, baby!" I returned my attention to my little girl patiently waiting in the back seat.

"Okay, Mommy!" she shouted back in her little voice.

We approached the front door of the daycare and rang the bell like we did each morning. Ms. Dawkins, Dylan's favorite teacher, happened to be walking from the main office and saw us waiting to get in. She had a huge smile on her face as she always did when she saw Dylan in the morning. Dylan got so excited that she began banging on the glass door with her little hands and jump up and down as if that would make Ms. Dawkins walk faster to let us in. Ms. Dawkins finally reached the door and as soon as she opened it to let us in, Dylan ran right into her arms.

"Ms. D! Ms. D!" Dylan shouted. Ms. Dawkins returned the excitement of Dylan's energetic greeting by embracing my baby with a warm hug and laughter. The care that Ms. Dawkins and the rest of the staff always provided Dylan made me feel relieved and confident in the services that the center offered. It was challenging enough to have to leave my daughter with strangers everyday while I worked, but knowing she was in the best of care got me through each day.

Geneya Singleton

After Dylan and I greeted the other staff members and children, we walked to her class full of other vibrant little angels. Ms. Dawkins gave me the go ahead to give Dylan a big hug and kiss and to go about my day. Back down the hall I went to get to my car and return to my conversation with Marcus. As I started the ignition, I had a split second thought of contemplation. Should I even call him back? I was sure he was expecting it, but maybe in a way that was demanding and not anticipated.

Snap out of it, Ava! I thought to myself. Here you go again, overthinking things and making unnecessary and most likely false assumptions. The ride to work was going to be short so there wouldn't be much time for him to get excited about the returned call anyways. Oh, forget it. I wanted to hear that sexy voice anyways. I'd just call.

"You kept me waiting much longer than I preferred." I heard through the speakers in my car. A deep but calm voice circulated through the entire vehicle and appeared to ricochet off of the doors and straight into my heart.

"It wasn't that long," I replied.

"Longer than I would normally allow, but you are in the learning process, so there is much more time for improvements." Marcus stated.

At this time, I was so confused emotionally and mentally. I was not sure how to take in this unique introduction to our new friendship. Marcus had been making statements that in a way should have been alarming to me, but somehow made me want more of it.

"I apologize. It won't happen again," I committed.

"Good girl," he replied once again. I was on my way out of the conversation into yet another moment of thought but before I could leave, Marcus began speaking again. "So, did you get your baby girl off to school okay?" he asked.

"Yes, I did. Thank you for asking," I said.

"Of course," Marcus replied. "Now, tell me a little about yourself. What is your favorite color, favorite food, favorite song, and what do you like to do in your spare time?"

"My favorite color is red…" Before I could move on to the next question, Marcus let out what sounded like a slight moan or an intrigued spark of curiosity.

"Why red?" he asked.

"Because it's bright, bold, and passionate, like me," I answered. "Red stands out above every color in the rainbow," I added sarcastically. "Like me."

"Confidence is a stain that the world couldn't wipe off if they tried." Marcus added. "I like that in you."

I smiled and proceeded to the next question. "My favorite food is lasagna.

I love that you get a warm layer of mixed, but consistent confusion with each bite," I explained.

"Let me guess, like you?" Marcus asked.

"Definitely like me," I responded with an unnecessary tone of confidence. "My favorite song?" I asked. "I can't say that I have a favorite song. I love all genres of music. I particularly love jazz. It can be so relaxing and sensual. Like me." Marcus let out a slight chuckle. I could tell he had been enjoying our conversation so far.

"When will I have the pleasure of taking you out on a date?" he asked.

I was almost hesitant to answer with anything other than a date and time. He had made it clear several times that all requests made by him should be fulfilled with a time sensitive approach.

Besides, deep down inside I couldn't wait to be with him for some one-on-one time. He was in full character when we met at the auto body shop with his small audience of Stan the mechanic and was certainly enjoying the privilege of hiding behind the phone right now. I would love to put him in the spotlight where it would be just the two of us in person, raw, and uncensored, conversations and whatever else we could...

Oh, snap out of it, Ava! I thought to myself.

"How about this coming Saturday?" I finally answered.

"Saturday is perfect!" Marcus said with excitement and confidence as if he knew I would accept his date invitation. "Where shall I take you?" he asked.

"I've always wanted to visit this local restaurant. I've been told that they make the best salmon and pasta dishes around. It's called Melanie's," I said. "I see their commercials all the time." Besides, I was a fat girl at heart, who had memorized the voiceovers for just about every food commercial there was.

"What time shall I pick you up?" Marcus asked.

"You tell me. You're the one in charge all of the time," I said sarcastically, but low key wanting to hear how he would have the evening planned for us from beginning to end. I didn't feel quite ready to date again, but I needed this outing so badly. I was a mother most of my available time and really missed having adult conversations and time.

"Good answer, sweetheart," he said. "According to your paperwork from the shop, you're just about twenty minutes from me. I'll arrive to sweep you off of your feet around 6 p.m. Please be ready on time and wear something red. I'll call you when I am exactly nine and a half minutes away from you," he informed me.

"Why nine and a half minutes?" I asked curiously.

"Nine minutes to anticipate my arrival, and thirty seconds to catch your breath."

I wasn't really sure how to respond at this point, but I could feel my excitement increasing by the minute. This man had such a rare personality. It was as if he was reading my mind. I mean, I surely had not been thinking of any of this. Well, maybe a little. Every word he'd spoken since the first day seemed so rehearsed but flowed so naturally. I decided to stop questioning everything and just enjoy the ride.

"Yes sir, I'll be ready for your arrival," I said.

"And what else?" Marcus asked in anticipation and with a slight tone of disappointment.

"I'll be wearing the richest shade of red I can find," I added.

"And?" he asked.

"And I will remember to catch my breath," I concluded.

"Good girl," he said. "Have you arrived to work yet?"

I hadn't even realized that I was subconsciously operating my vehicle. I had gotten so thrown by our conversation, that I actually had arrived at work and even parked my car without realizing it. I couldn't wait to get inside and tell my boss all about my new friend. She would be so intrigued by his unique personality, and I was sure she'd be surprised that I had even given someone the time of day.

Geneya Singleton

Audrey and I had worked together for a few years now and had become so close. We knew just about everything about one another. She knew that I had developed major trust issues since my divorce and spent most of my days avoiding men, if not deliberately chasing them away. There was just something about Marcus that made me want to stay this time and let down my guard. I'm sure she would have a million questions about this one but this time I was ready to finally answer them. "Yes, I am at work now. I hope the rest of your morning is peaceful and full of much needed rest," I said.

"Thank you, sweetheart." Marcus replied. "I plan to go to the gym, have some breakfast and then sleep for a few hours. I have to work again tonight. I hope to hear from you at some point before I head to work?" he asked.

"Oh, absolutely," I said. "Just send me a text message when you wake up. I promise to respond."

"Good girl," he said. "Have a great day at work. I'll be thinking of you," Marcus added.

"I'm sure you will," I sarcastically responded.

"Don't be a bad girl now, sweetheart. You were doing so well." Marcus said.

"Don't you want me to be bad sometimes?" I asked in an innocent but flirtatious tone.

"Oh yes, but only when given permission," he replied. Somehow, I understood his permission to misbehave better than I probably should have.

"Understood, sir," I remorsefully acknowledged.

"Very good girl," Marcus said, this time slowly releasing the beginning of his sentence as if to acknowledge my obedience and reward me at the same time.

"Thank you, sir. I'm looking forward to speaking with you later today," I said.

"I know you are," he replied. "Have a great day on purpose for me," he added just before we ended our call.

"You as well," I replied.

As I approached the bank, I walked into the waiting lines outside. Mondays were pretty busy. The day consisted of frustrated customers who had spent more money than they had available in their bank accounts over the weekend. They somehow would hold the employees accountable for their own mismanagement of funds. The amount of people with overdraft refund demands would fill the lobby. We would spend so much time educating each customer on how to properly utilize their finances and offer them various options to protect them from those lovely overdraft fees, but it seemed no matter how much we talked to them, they would repeat the same behaviors.

A group effort of morning greetings rang through my ears as I got closer to the crowd.

"Good morning, everyone! We will be opening the doors shortly," I assured them as I made my way through the crowd blocking the doors. I rang the bell to gain entrance and start my lovely day. I was still feeling warm inside from the early morning conversations with that firefighter. I had the biggest smile on my face. As my manager Audrey approached the doors to let me in.

She stopped a few feet back and yelled through the glass doors, "How can I help you?" to sarcastically imply that my identity must have changed overnight because she had never seen such a smile on my face. I couldn't help but to show it. Besides, I deserved it after spending so much of my life frowning inside and out.

As she finally turned the locks to open the doors for me, I greeted her with the loudest, most cheerful, "Good morning!"

"What? You got some dicks last night?"

I attempted to correct her by saying, "Don't you mean dick?"

"No, I meant the plural. You know you're a hoe!" she accused, as she let out a burst of loud laughter.

"Shut up!" I demanded with a chuckle as I walked through the bank's lobby by her side.

"Spill it!" she aggressively commanded as she stopped walking abruptly, yanked me into her office, and quickly slammed the door behind us. All I could do was smile and cover my irresistible desire to giggle.

"Bitch!" I started out before dumping my exclusively newfound secret on her. "I met a guy a yesterday! He is amazing! He is a firefighter and oh so fine! He's tall, fair skinned, and with dimples that you could spot ten miles away! He is single, I think…" and it was at that very moment that I interrupted my own story and excitement as I realized I had failed to ask Marcus if he was seeing anyone. How could I have been so caught up in his presence and conversation that I'd forgotten to ask that very important, deal-breaking question?

"Are you still with me, you little hussy?"

I realized that I had drifted off into thought again. I quickly snapped back into reality as I was so rudely ushered back into the realm of the gossip and excitement.

Fire Without a Flame

"Oh yes. Sorry, Audrey. I'm here. I just realized that I'd forgotten to ask my new ever-so-fine friend what his relationship status is."

If it was anything close to what I was imagining, he was player of the year. There was no way in this large world of desperation that we live in that he was single and available. Although I had big hopes for us, I would just mentally and emotionally prepare myself to use him for late night and early morning oral communication, the kind where you use your mouth but not for words.

"Are you going to finish your story or not?" Audrey asked me.

I snapped out of my X-rated moment of thinking to see her with her arms folded with that Cuban zirconia ring bulging from the clasp of her frustrated hands. Whatever turn my social life was going to take, I prayed to God that I wouldn't end up with a cheapskate who would think so little of me to propose with plastic glass glued to a soda can flip-top. Of course, I'd never tell Audrey that her much-admired diamond ring was no diamond at all.

"Oh, where was I?" I asked with a sly smirk displayed across my round face while still staring in the direction of that cheap ass ring.

"You were saying that he may or may not be single and something about his goofy ass smile." Audrey was the queen of sarcasm and the head bitch of jealousy. Her man never smiled. I mean, if I were him, I wouldn't either. He had the darkest, most dry face I had ever seen in my life. I love my brothers and all of the melanin that covered their temples, but Audrey's man suffered from poor hygiene issues and had lost a few rounds of battle with eczema. He had one missing tooth on the side and

69

his breath reeked of ten day old steak and onions, which somehow always managed to seep through the doorway in his mouth by way of that missing tooth. He wore a gallon of cologne. The cheap kind that you found at the dollar store. He really had nothing to smile about so why wouldn't she be envious of my Marcus already?

"Yes, girl," I quickly returned to my romantic gossip. "Remember yesterday when I went to take my car back to that poor excuse of a mechanic, Stan?"

"Oh, yes! I remember!" Audrey replied.

"Well there I was, standing in the lobby complaining to Stan about the shoddy work his employees had done on my car and explaining why I had returned for service so soon after my last visit, when out of nowhere this fine being I now know as Marcus interjected himself into our conversation. He asked if he could assist Stan with locating my paperwork. He wore a paramedic's uniform, so I assumed he was a customer like myself."

"Why was he asking questions anyway?" Audrey asked in her high pitched tone of annoyance as she interrupted my story.

"Well, I'm getting there now," I said. "Naturally, I hated the way a man looked, walked, stood, and breathed since my divorce. But, girl, there was just something about this man. His presence demanded my attention. I behaved as rudely as I could to discontinue and reject his advances but to no avail. I just gave in. His charm made me feel like a little girl again. His smile made me want to give him children, and his print... Well, let's just say he got my attention."

"You're such a sucker!" Audrey shouted.

"I know I am when it comes to large prints and even bigger smiles," I replied. "Listen, he could have a kidney or two. I'm not using them anyways," I said being silly. "Well, he did help locate my file and a few pieces to my broken heart. We have plans this coming weekend for our first date and I'm so excited!"

Audrey just stared in my direction with her dominant eye focused on me. Audrey had one lazy eye that she claimed was the result of stress, but the way she expressed herself verbally to any and everyone, I'm pretty sure her ugly fiancé probably smacked her around quite a few times just to remind her who was boss. I didn't condone domestic violence of any form, but I had witnessed Audrey speaking to him in public on several occasions. She was so demeaning and condescending towards him and she paid no attention or expressed concern about whomever was nearby to see her disrespect unfold. Her fiancé was definitely not the most masculine of men, but for God's sake he deserved some respect.

"So where are you love birds headed?" she asked as if she was suddenly rooting for my new friend and I.

"I'm thinking that new seafood place downtown that everyone has been raving about."

"That sounds great! Their food is really delicious," Audrey agreed. "I hope this one works out for you so we can double date one day," she added.

"That would be nice," I said and pretended to show interest. I would never in my life be caught out in public with Mr. Dry Skin and Ms. Say Anything.

"Well, unfortunately it's time to open the doors to let in the waiting crowd," Audrey said as she headed over to the front doors of the bank.

I scurried over to the lobby to greet the antsy customers as they entered the bank two at a time through

Geneya Singleton

the double doors. It was the bank's policy to have an employee available to greet customers as they entered and exited the bank during business hours. They felt it would display a sense of appreciation and value and somehow deter robberies. I think it was all a ploy to mimic a large local retailer's customer service protocol and a few neighborhood competitors. It was a quality idea but held little true value seeing as how it wasn't genuine, in my opinion. It was a way for the employees to tackle the customers and solicit them for new business relationships. Every branch employee played a vital role in meeting corporate goals by offering bank customers enticing borrowing opportunities. There was just something about not being able to decline a sweet deal. when it is up close and personal. It was a way to drive sales.

I was one of the top performing sales representatives in my region. I was blessed with a natural gift of gab, so it was never a challenge for me to gain the trust of any customer and sell them the bells and whistles of life. Honesty and straightforwardness was my secret to success. I would normally face a typical Monday morning with a dull sense of the first day of the week blues, but today was different. Today, I felt alive.

Nothing would come between the excitement and new sense of hope I was feeling. I would spend the next few days living by the clock, counting down to the day of my first date with Marcus. Each day after Monday was like the first. I was all smiles and positive energy. Marcus pushed me through the days with early morning calls and random sweet text messages each day. He was starting to grow on me, but I was still taking my time and proceeding with caution. A small part of me wondered if there was an ulterior motive. Was I another number in his little

72

Fire Without a Flame

black book? It honestly didn't matter at this point. We were going places, and I was surely down for the ride.

Scintillation

It was another early Friday morning, around the scheduled time that Marcus would call me. I would always let the phone go one extra ring with each call from him so as not to appear as desperate as I had really been feeling.

"Hi, handsome!" I greeted him with an excited tone.

"Well, good morning, beautiful," Marcus replied. "You sound very excited and welcoming this morning," he added.

"Well, I may be a little excited," I admitted.

"And why is that?" he asked.

"Well, for three wonderful reasons," I said.

"I'm listening," said Marcus.

"Well, for starters, it's Friday! Second, I'm working half a day today, and finally," I added, "tomorrow is Saturday!"

"Well, for as long as I've been alive Saturday has always followed Friday," Marcus said sarcastically. I decided to give him a pass today since I was in such a good mood, so I disregarded him and proceeded with my excitement.

"Well, tomorrow is definitely Saturday but it's a special kind of Saturday," I expressed.

"And what would make tomorrow's Saturday such a special Saturday out of all that have come before it?" Marcus asked.

"Well, I was going on a date with a special friend," I replied. "But he and I just broke up due to an overdose of sarcasm. It was just way too way too much for a woman of my caliber."

We shared a few moments of silence before he responded in the sexiest tone I'd ever heard.

"Oh, that's too bad. I'm really sorry to hear that. With the level of excitement you were just expressing, it appeared as if this guy was pretty special to you and now he's gone just like that? He was probably the best thing that ever happened to you. Maybe you should have a little more patience with people. Or maybe, just maybe you need a spanking for speaking to Daddy like that. Also, maybe you should apologize within the next ten seconds to avoid further consequence."

"Excuse me?" I replied in total shock and disbelief of how this conversation had taken a sudden change in direction. *What the hell is happening here?* I thought to myself.

Before I could ask myself another question, Marcus interrupted, "Five seconds left."

I let out a confused but somehow intrigued giggle. I wanted to play this game or whatever it was with him. I figured if he was bold enough to role play, surely I shouldn't let him play alone.

"I'm sorry..." I started out.

"Good girl," Marcus replied.

"I'm sorry that you think somehow you're in charge," I finished.

"What was that, little girl?" Marcus asked.

My mind began to race for a second. He was referring to me as a "little girl" now. I could feel my body beginning to tremble slightly inside.

Should I go further and risk treading the troubled waters? I was curious to see what kind of consequences awaited me on the other side of this conversation. I was a bit nervous, but I was feeling kinky at the same time. Marcus had awakened something in me that I hadn't felt in a long time. I was even surprised that my lady senses were fully functioning and active. Who was this man? How did he just land on my doorsteps like an answered prayer?

"Little girl?" he repeated. I was immediately summoned back to reality by Marcus's very direct demand for the return of my attention.

"Yes, sir?" I replied.

"Sir?" he inquired.

"Yes, sir Marcus?" I asked.

Geneya Singleton

"You will address me as Daddy unless otherwise instructed," he commanded. "We have a lot of work to do with you I see," he said.

Now I was completely confused but had the highest desire to stick around for more. Or should I make a run for it? I didn't want to go too far. Or did I?

Fuck it! I thought to myself. *You've been living in an emotional shelter for the past few years. Go out and have some fun!*

"Yes, Daddy," I replied. "I apologize for speaking out of turn and my deliberate disrespect and disregard for authority. It won't happen again."

"Good girl. Now listen to me carefully," he instructed. "Tomorrow is indeed a special day. It is the fourth day of the best days of your life."

I was unclear on the counting of my "best days" that Marcus had come up with, so I interjected, "The fourth day, sir? I mean, Daddy."

"Yes," he replied. "The first day is the day you entered into this world. The second day is the day that you gave birth to your daughter. The third day is the day I entered into your life and tomorrow will be the fourth day," he explained. "A day I promise you shall remember for the rest of your natural life."

I was in complete awe and at a loss for words. I had no rebuttal appropriate enough, let alone permissible to a man who spoke with such authority, determination, confidence, and straightforwardness.

"Little girl, are you with me?" Marcus asked in a tone that suggested he was just as surprised that I remained on the telephone fully participating in this very unique conversation.

"Yes, I'm here," I replied. "I'm looking forward to tomorrow. You appear to have all of the details planned out. I appreciate your due diligence and efforts in ensuring the day goes as perfect as I am imagining it will be."

"When I execute any plans, I put my name behind, everything becomes flawless and most memorable," Marcus said. "I only ask that you allow me to be in control at all times. I know that this is just the beginning for us, but I am asking in advance for your trust. I need you to be ready for me and as relaxed as possible. The day will be like none other that you've experienced in your life and this is my promise to you. Please be ready by 6 p.m. Please wear a very lightly scented perfume. Please also find a very deep shade of red lipstick and some very cheap black mascara.

Please wear a very small sized pair of earrings. Not too much foundation, if you do wear any makeup. And finally, tell no one of the requests I have just made of you."

Marcus' listing of demands and preferences had gone on for at least two minutes. I remained silent the whole time, just taking it all in. This was definitely a unique experience for me from the beginning. I developed a very strong desire to make my exit from this conversation and his life. I was unclear as to how far his rare and unusual characteristic traits and vivid imagination would take us or even if it was safe for us to continue. Hell, was it safe for me? Dylan would need me around for a very long time. She was so young. What if this Marcus was some sort of serial killer? He sure didn't look like one, but then again what did one even look like before the murder weapon was in their hands?

Geneya Singleton

"Did I lose you, little girl?" Marcus interjected during my mental drift. Only this time I thought maybe I should stay a little longer in my thoughts to begin to dissect and rationalize all of the crazy shit this man had been throwing my way.

"I'll call you right back, Marcus," I responded. And just like that, I ended the call.

I sat for a few minutes in much needed silence. *Okay think, honey.* I began coaching myself. Who the hell was I kidding? There is no damn way I could even begin to tackle this crazy shit alone. I needed my best friend, Salene.

I was sure she would tell me to pack my shit and go immediately. She was the more mentally stable one between the two of us, and she was cutthroat and always straight to the point. But then again, Marcus had clearly instructed me to not share the details of our date with anyone. What if he had some sick ass ability to read my mind and detect dishonesty? He would surely take my life then.

Oh, snap out of it, Ava! I thought to myself. How in the world would he be able to read my mind if I never called him again? Or would I? That's it! I couldn't dial Salene's number fast enough.

"Hey, girl!" Salene had answered on the first ring.

"Salene!!" I shouted into the other end of the phone.

"Oh God, what's wrong?" she asked.

"It's the new guy," I stated.

"The firefighter?" she asked.

"Yes, girl!"

"What did he do?" she asked in a curious but 'if you have hurt my best friend already, I'll burn your entire house down' tone.

"Nothing is really wrong. Or it might be really wrong or unusually right," I said.

Salene took a deep breath before she let out a very confused, "What the hell are you talking about, Ava?"

"Well," I started. "We are having our first date tomorrow."

"Oh wonderful!" Salene shouted. "And you're unhappy about that? You should be excited that someone finally came along and is ready take your tired ass out for a good time!"

"Girl, will you shut up and listen to me!" I had to interrupt Salene and completely stop her in her tracks. She had a habit of activating her personal "crazy" start button and I've yet to uncover her stop button.

"Okay, okay I'm listening!" Salene pleaded.

"I just finished a call with him, and he began to break down the details of how our date would go."

"Okay, sounds like we have a man that knows what he wants and has entered into the friendship with purpose and good intentions." Salene was on her way again into whatever realm of personal opinion that she lived in.

"Salene, may I finish?" I begged.

"Oh, of course. I'm sorry," she said.

"Now, as I am fully attentive to Marcus' plans for the date, I'm suddenly shocked by the specificity of it all. He starts out by telling me how I should be punctual. Nothing particularly wrong with that. He then begins making very particular requests about how I should

Geneya Singleton

present myself to him upon his arrival. He says he would like for me to wear something red in color, small sized earrings, light makeup, and to have on a softly scented perfume."

"I am still waiting for the problem," Salene interrupted.

"You don't find those requests unusual?" I asked.

"Well, certainly unusual; but not life threatening. You've got to learn to live a little, Ava. You have been single for so long, you are totally out of the loop."

"So, you mean to tell me this is the new norm in the world of dating?" I asked.

"Well, I wouldn't say the new norm; just the norm for the vibrant and risky. Neither of which apply to you."

"Oh hush!" I said.

"Unless you are about to tell me that he requested the left kidney of your second born, may I suggest you go with the flow and enjoy the ride? Listen, if he ends up being a serial killer and we find your ass in a trunk with red lipstick smudges around your neck, just know that Dylan will be in good hands and you've lived a great and memorable life."

"Salene!" I shouted.

"Oh, I'm just kidding!" she said. "Go be curious with your weird firefighter. It's just a date. If you don't like him or this date, there is an option to 'return-to-sender' and you can go on with your life as if you've never met him. Listen, let's create a safe word or text. If you feel uncomfortable at any point during the date, text me the word 'extinguisher' and send me your location. I will have the entire homicide unit on scene within five minutes."

Fire Without a Flame

"Homicide?" I asked.

"Hell yes! I'll kill his ass with my bare hands within three minutes, so that will leave one minute to clean up the evidence and another minute to wait for homicide to arrive."

I let out what had to be the biggest, loudest, fit of laughter there ever was. Deep down inside I knew she was not kidding around.

"Now get off of this phone with me and give him a call back because if I know you like I know I do, you ended the call abruptly as the rude and scary individual you are." We both laughed because we clearly knew one another better than anyone else on the face of the earth.

"Okay, Salene. I'll give him a call back. Thanks for the talk."

"Of course! That's what friends are for."

We ended our call, and I felt much better than I did before we began it. She was right. Even though the conversation between Marcus and I had been very much unique and slightly uncomfortable at times, it could very well be harmless. It had been a while since I'd had anything remotely close to what I was experiencing with him. Maybe I should just enjoy the ride. I reached for my phone again and slowly began to scan my call history to return his call that I had so rudely interrupted. I could feel my heartrate begin to increase. The phone seemed to ring much more loudly this time around. I was feeling very anxious.

"Hey, beautiful. Is everything okay?" Marcus asked as soon as he answered the call.

"Yes, I'm sorry. I must've been driving through an area with poor reception. I called you back as soon as I could." I was pretty good at covering up my feelings whenever I needed to. How would I even begin to explain to him that he had made me slightly nervous and uncomfortable?

"Oh, for a second I thought you intentionally disconnected the call," Marcus said. "I thought maybe I had been moving a little too fast for you?"

"Oh, not at all!" I said in the most untruthful way.

"Well, if I ever make you uncomfortable, please promise me you will let me know immediately and not leave me?"

"Leave you?" I asked curiously. We were just two friends that were in the very premature phase of our relationship. What the hell was this guy talking about? "Okay, I will definitely inform you if I feel you are moving at a rate that makes me uncomfortable in any way. I'm very outspoken and straightforward at all times."

"Sounds good," he replied.

I was definitely portraying myself as whoever I wanted to be to Marcus, but I damn sure was not kidding myself. I had a poor habit of sparing the feelings of others while sacrificing my own happiness. I'd always been popular among people and could never lower my score by calling a person on their bullshit, so I remained full of it myself.

"Good girl."

There he went with this good girl shit. Why couldn't he just address me by my name? I mean, sometimes it was really cute and felt adventurous and scandalous, but at some point I would just like to hear my own damn name.

Fire Without a Flame

"Thank you, sir." I responded. I decided to play along just to see where these charades would lead us.

"Now, as I was saying before our call was disconnected, I will arrive at the designated time specified previously. I am looking forward to spending quality time with you, and I am so excited for you to see all of the surprises that await you tomorrow evening."

"As am I," I replied. My mind began to wander again. I hoped this man was not some psychopath that lived in the basement of his mother's home and collected shards of glass and cutting knives for fun.

"Well, I'm off to get some rest before my shift tonight," Marcus said. "Have a great day at work, and I will speak with you before I head out later today."

"I will. Thank you. I hope you get as much uninterrupted rest as you need, sir." I added.

I could almost feel his warm smile seeping through the phone connection. The call was complete, and I didn't feel as nearly uncomfortable as I had before. My day would have to go well with all of the schoolgirl butterflies I felt in my stomach, along with the excitement of what tomorrow would bring. Was this really happening? Had I finally found the one? Or had he found me? I hoped my dreams had finally come true. Even if this was a temporary exchange of energy, I'd already committed myself to riding this thing until the wheels fell off. And him too, on regular occasions.

I let out a fresh-pot little girl giggle. Who was I kidding? I couldn't wait to give it up to Marcus. He could have the cake and eat it too. I never understood the whole ninety-day waiting game. If you like someone and you know full well you share some form of chemistry with them, what was the waiting period all about? Was it some sort of trial period like a cheap insurance plan? I never liked to waste anyone's time or have mine wasted. If Marcus played his cards right, he would certainly understand the validity of the chemistry between us. If it was this heavy over the phone, surely the bedroom would speak even louder.

Ava, come on girl. You've spent more time thinking about tomorrow than you have actually preparing for it, I chastised myself. I had just realized that I did not have all of Marcus' requirements for our upcoming date readily available and needed to get to the store as soon as possible. I knew just the place to go and would head there right after work.

The workday had been one of the most peaceful days I'd had in a while. I mean, I did encounter a few irate customers and some annoying coworkers, but I had so much excitement and anticipation inside of me that everything that came my way seemed to roll right off of me like a bead of sweat from a fine, tall, dark, and handsome Marcus. I mean, man. He had already consumed a great deal of my mental capacity. The very thought of him made me quiver like a bare-skinned swim through an arctic river.

Pace yourself, Ava. I quickly sent a reminder to my brain and made sure a carbon copy was sent to my heart. Sure, this feeling had been long overdue, but I'd broken every track record in terms of mistaking lust for love. I didn't love the guy of course, but I could feel my heart getting much more ahead of my brain, and I hadn't even let off the starting pistol yet.

I half-ass worked my shift. I was sure I closed at least one loan and typed up a few documents, but mostly I fantasized about Marcus. I wondered what he had had in store for us tomorrow. Was he going to blindfold me and take me to a faraway place full of romance and kinky behavior? I wouldn't be able to contain the suspense of the unknown much longer. My short shift ended and eagerly rushed off to get to my princess. She would be spending the weekend with her favorite aunt while I borrowed a day or two of mommy time with Marcus, so I wanted to make sure she and I got some time together beforehand.

I had planned to take her to her favorite ice cream shop nearby. Dylan loved the self-serve option. I would allow her to make the biggest, messiest "scream" bowl, as she would call it. I arrived at Dylan's daycare, and as I parked my car I was startled by the very loud sound of a fire truck's horn as it passed me by. The small shock quickly turned into chills that ran through my body. As the truck sped by, I could only imagine the heroic men that sat inside.

My thoughts immediately shifted back to Marcus and our date tomorrow. I would love for him to wear that uniform of his when he arrived to pick me up. Maybe I should call and ask him?

Oh, come on, Ava! I thought to myself. He would think you have lost all your mental abilities if you ever asked him anything remotely close to that. The thought departed just as quickly as it had introduced itself to my mind.

Since I was a teenager, I'd really had a thing for men in uniform. I shouldn't have even been old enough to conjure up such thoughts at that age, but after a school field trip to a prison, seeing so many fine men wearing rich shades of navy blue with shiny badges and midnight black guns, I knew that one day I would have to be in some form of relationship with a man in a uniform that represented authority or heroism to me. Maybe that one day had arrived. Sooner than I thought, but at no better time than now.

As I approached the doors of the daycare center, I could see Dylan's class through the glass as they were returning from a bathroom trip. I saw the smile on Dylan's face all the way down the hall as she headed back to her class. She was so happy and oh so perfect to me. I rang the doorbell and within a few seconds was greeted by the owner of the center. I had only met her personally once before during my enrollment process for Dylan. She appeared friendly the first time we'd met, but I had seen her a few times since then and she would barely part her lips to greet many of the parents as they entered and exited her establishment daily.

My assumption was that she presented herself one way to acquire the new business and then returned to her normalcy of rude behavior once she obtained it. She didn't run the business herself. She had the foresight to hire some of the most prestigious and professional staff members to represent the center in her absence. Maybe she was here today just to collect tuition payments and head off to her weekly hair appointments and shoe shopping excursions. She was always so well dressed, and her hair was always so full of bouncing curls; not one strand would be out of place ever. It was safe to say that the cover of the book can never tell the story. You have to read each page, one word at a time.

As I approached Dylan's classroom, I could hear the voices of the children singing their end of the day song. The song included lyrics that encouraged the children to clean up their play area and get ready to say goodbye to their friends. Dylan loved to sing and clap and dance to just about any tune. She was musically inspired by all genres of music.

I entered her classroom and as soon as she laid eyes on me, she quickly ran into my arms while shouting, "Mommy!"

It was one of the best, warmest feelings I had ever felt. Each hug represented the innocence of my little toddler with a combination of gratitude. She relied so much on me for her safety and happiness. I was so ever grateful that she chose me to be her mommy.

"Hi baby!" I shouted to return her greeting. "Mommy missed you so much today! Are you ready to go and get some ice cream?"

"'Scream?" Dylan replied.

"Yes, princess! We are going to go and make the biggest mess that we can and then eat it all up!" Dylan started clapping her tiny hands together as though to agree to the mess-making ice cream party. I knew she was just two years old, but I was pretty convinced that she understood everything I said to her. Admiring the big smile still present across her little cheeks, I quickly grabbed her belongings and we said our goodbyes as we left.

As soon as we arrived at the parlor, Dylan immediately began to grab the straps of her car seat and kick her little feet back and forth one leg at a time. She knew exactly where she was, and she was determined to get inside and dive into our 'Mommy and Me' Friday tradition. The girls that worked in the parlor knew Dylan by name and would make us feel so welcomed each time we visited. We entered the busy shop and, after exchanging a few greetings, we headed to our favorite booth. Dylan enjoyed sitting by the window so she could

Geneya Singleton

see the faces of people walking by. I personally think she took it as an opportunity to show off her frozen treat, but who was I to judge my baby girl? Dylan somehow always managed to get more ice cream on her clothes and face then she did in her mouth. After spending some time at the parlor, we cleaned up our team effort of a mess and headed out to drop Dylan off to her favorite aunt's house. I was going to miss seeing her beautiful face for a few days, but I was overdue for the break.

We arrived at my sister Sophie's house, which was just a few minutes from our home. She was the youngest of my siblings and she loved Dylan like she was her own. Dylan recognized the neighborhood as soon as we arrived. She began clapping and singing her "Auntie" song that she had made up a few months ago. She would sing, "Auntie is my auntie and I love my auntie." This rendition would continue on until she was face-to-face with her auntie. My sister thoroughly enjoyed this toddler orchestrated musical, of course. It made her feel like she was the only relative Dylan knew and loved. I admittedly enjoyed it myself because I was so amazed at how quickly Dylan was growing into the various stages of childhood. Each milestone was so unique.

We exited the vehicle and approached my sister's front door. Sophie was my favorite sibling. She had class and style much like my own. Her home was uniquely decorated and carefully crafted from the floors to the ceiling. While I had an eye for fashion, she was an interior designer. Dylan loved to ring Sophie's doorbell whenever we visited. She would find so much humor in the rhythm of the chimes and would giggle hysterically. She also anticipated Sophie's approach once the bell ringing began. After Dylan released the doorbell with the second ring, she opened her eyes really wide, focused on the door, and listened quietly so she could hear Sophie's footsteps draw near. Suddenly the doorknob began to turn and Dylan focused her eyes on me, and then back on the front door. I could feel her heart rate increase from excitement. The door was beginning to open. Before I could let Dylan down from my arms, she leaped towards the front door just in time for Sophie to catch her midair. Sophie and I broke out into laughter. I was pretty sure we were both processing the ideas of disbelief and relief at once. I couldn't believe that Dylan had built up so much anxiety to greet her favorite aunt that she would risk it all just to get to Sophie. Boy, were we thankful that Sophie's reflexes were on point on that day.

"Hi, Dilly!" Sophie shouted.

"Auntie, auntie, I love my auntie!" The musical rendition continued. All I could do was smile and nod my head to the toddler tune.

"Niecy, Niecy, I love my Niecy," Sophie sang back. Before you knew it, there was a full concert being performed on the front porch.

"Listen," I interrupted. "If you two are done with this one night only performance, here are Dylan's bags, here is a kiss, and here is my back as I am making a run for my freedom!" I chuckled as I made good on each one of those promises and headed down the stairs in the direction of my car. "Mommy loves you, Dylan!" I yelled as I hit the last step that positioned me beside my car door.

"Well goodbye to you too!" Sophie yelled down. I just turned around and smiled. She smiled back because she knew I was very excited to be free from parental responsibilities even if it was just for a few days.

Geneya Singleton

When I started my ignition, it felt different. I took a quick glimpse into my rearview mirror and was instantly reminded that I could play my music as loud as I wanted to since there was no Dylan napping in the back. I shuffled through the playlist on my music app and found the perfect song to blast as I drove off into the night feeling free!

Once I arrived home, I completed my daily routine of quickly sorting through the mail to look for any envelopes worth opening.

I was so used to getting bills and late notices from just about everywhere. I would frantically search through the pile of unwanted reminders in hopes of one day finding an overdue payment from the state for child support. That bastard was ten months behind. The monthly support that he was ordered to pay was well under three-hundred dollars, and he had the audacity to fall behind.

Today was not payday, I confirmed as I had reached the bottom of my pile.

Oh well, I thought to myself. I still had so much more to look forward to this weekend. I headed toward the kitchen to my beautiful wine rack and pulled out a bottle of my favorite cabernet. I loved red wine. Well, only dry palates. As I grew older, my taste buds had certainly changed. That sweet stuff gave me the most egregious form of heartburn and left me feeling like I was sipping on a kid's juice box, only out of a very fancy wine glass. I filled my glass to the brim and headed up the stairs to run a nice hot bubble bath. I stopped by the dinner table to grab my favorite scented candle to add to the ambiance. There was just something about the smell of sandalwood that made me feel so relaxed and free. Once I made my way out of the last layer of my work attire, I grabbed my wireless speaker, powered it on, and increased the volume to the max. I shuffled through my playlist once again and decided on the smooth sound of jazz.

Glass in hand, I dipped my big toe into the mountain of bubbles for a quick temperature check. It was perfect. I submerged the rest of my tired body into the bathtub and released a deep sigh of relief into the room. The neighborhood was quiet, and the sun had begun to disappear into the sky. I took a sip of my wine and savored the taste it left on my brown sugar colored lips. Life was good. As the speaker emitted beautiful notes of saxophones and pianos, I gave myself permission to totally let go. I rested my glass on the ledge of the bathtub and closed my eyes for a few minutes. The lights were low, and the candle illuminated against the ceiling. I was finally free.

After a few minutes of this wonderful bliss, I began to think about my date with Marcus tomorrow. I mentally scanned my closets to see what I could wear for him on our first date. I immediately remembered the beautiful red dress that Salene had bought me for my last birthday. She knew red was my favorite color and had instructed me to wear it when I was feeling like myself again after my divorce.

Wouldn't that be the perfect dress to wear for Marcus? I thought. What better way to say "I'm moving the fuck on" than to pull out that fiery red dress and wear it for a fireman? It was settled! I'd wear that dress with my black leather thigh high boots and a black blazer and clutch. I had the perfect silver studded earrings to wear with the matching bracelet and ring. Oh, this would definitely be a night to remember! I couldn't contain my excitement. Since he was already on my mind, I decided I should send

Marcus a text message. He should've been at work by now and thinking of me anyway. Or at least he had better.

Good evening, handsome, I typed and pressed send.

Right away, my notification light illuminated my phone.

Well good evening, beautiful.

I was of a fair brown complexion, but I was sure anyone could see the red blush surrounding my cheeks as I read the message. I could feel his energy through the phone as if he were sitting right next to me.

I hope your evening is going well and the fire bells are not ringing too loudly, I responded.

The only bells that are going off at this moment, are the ones in my head and in my heart as I await and try to contain the excitement of seeing your beautiful face again tomorrow, he sent back.

At this point, I was feeling a slight buzz from the almost emptied glass of wine. The cabernet was saying to believe him, but my right mind had detected a pinch of bullshit mixed with game. But I thought, what the heck? I'd just go along for the ride.

Well, that was really sweet of you to say. I cannot wait to see your face either.

Do you have a minute to talk? he asked.

I most certainly do, I informed him.

The call came in almost immediately after that last message. I donned my sexy voice.

"Well hello, sir," I answered.

"Don't you mean Daddy?" he replied. I almost choked on the last drops of wine that I had tilted to the back of my throat with that question.

"Well, maybe I may mean that one day, just not today," I said.

Marcus sat in a few seconds of silence then let out a deep sigh of confidence and slight annoyance before he answered, "One day soon, sweetheart. Trust me."

I wasn't sure how to respond to that statement, so I just provided him with the scripted response he was looking for. "Yes, sir, I am quite sure."

"Are you ready for our date tomorrow?" he asked.

"Yes indeed, I am. I can't wait to enjoy some one-on-one time with you," I said.

"I feel the same," Marcus replied. "The entire evening will be full of surprises and great times."

"I'll hold you to that," I told him.

"I'm a man of my word and I ensure you, you will enjoy the evening," he promised.

"I believe you."

"I hope you do," he said. "I really put a lot of thought into preparing this evening for you, for us."

"I know you did. I can tell by the way you hold conversation that you put very serious energy into anything you do," I said.

"I do."

"What time should I be ready again?" I asked.

"Did you forget your instructions already?" Marcus asked.

"No, I didn't forget my instructions, sir. I just like the way you explain them to me, line by line."

"So, what you are saying is that you enjoy being naughty?" Marcus asked.

"I've broken a rule or two in my life," I said with the sexiest sarcasm I could muster.

"Oh, is that right?" he asked, returning the vibes I had just given off.

"Oh, it is," I continued. "Now would you please be so kind as to remind me of how this date shall go? ...Sir."

"I love how quickly you are catching on, little girl. You are making Daddy very proud to know you."

I felt a light flush of erotic sensation flow through me at that very moment. I thought for a second that I should slow things down because it was obvious that this guy was on cruise control with no option to permit me to navigate. I remembered of the advice that Salene had given me and decided to continue with the flow of events.

"Thank you, sir. I do aim to please."

"I've noticed that, little girl, and your good intentions have been duly noted. There are so many good things in store for you, if you come in quietly and have a seat. Basically, just enjoy the show. Understood?"

"Yes, sir," I confirmed.

"Here are your instructions once again. Please write them down if you must, just don't expect any mercy from me if you, for some reason, unfortunately misplace them or fail to follow them at any point. Are you ready?" Marcus asked.

"Indeed, I am, sir. Only I am completely submerged in a bathtub full of room temperature water and am too wet to retrieve a writing utensil. I will trust my own cognitive abilities to remember and process each set of instructions. At your desire, please state my instructions...Sir."

"Oh, little girl, if I were not on the clock at this very moment, you would be bent over across my lap and enduring the harshest spanking of your life."

I froze for a second. I was thinking I may have gone too far. What did he mean by spanking me? What kind of freak was this guy? I've already been a part of one emotionally abusive relationship in my life with Anthony, I would never be part of another in any form.

"Did I lose you little girl?"

"No, sir. I am here. I am just taking it all in."

He continued with his instructions. "I will arrive at your home at exactly six o'clock on the dot. You will be ready and will have on a small set of earrings, preferably the studded size. You will be wearing something red in color. You will aromatically draw in my attention with the most sensually, soft scent of your perfume You will greet me with a gentle hug, and I will return the greeting with a soft kiss on your forehead. We will then proceed to my vehicle and you will approach the passenger door ahead of me. I will then open your door and assist you into the vehicle. Once you are situated inside of the vehicle, I will proceed to the driver's side door, and you will then reach over and open the door for me. We will drive off into the evening to begin our date. Please ensure you make those few short minutes as memorable as possible because when you return to your place of residence you will not be the same as when you left."

Okay now, it was time for me to get the hell off of the phone with this man! What the fuck was he talking about? Was I being pimped out after dessert?

Geneya Singleton

Okay, stay cool, Ava!, I told myself. He's just a little different than the norm. The norm is what got you into single parenthood remember? "Okay, sir, I will remember every word. I promise," I said as I returned back from panic mode.

"Good girl. Now let me get back to work so I can hopefully finish my paperwork and sneak in a nap or two. I want to be as well rested as possible for tomorrow."

"I as well."

"I'll speak with you in the morning, beautiful," Marcus he told me.

"Goodnight, sir."

I disconnected the call and immediately dropped my phone onto the ivory colored tile floors of my bathroom. It was time for me to get out of the now cold bath water, get into some cozy pajamas, and surely get another glass of wine. I needed to relax as much as possible so that I could sleep like a baby, especially since I would possibly be getting treated like a wild animal tomorrow. I had to giggle at that thought myself. The walls were pretty thin in the homes in my neighborhood. I was sure my neighbors had a large drinking cup on the walls tonight. It was usually so quiet in my home and now I had a jazz band going and laughter. If this was the beginning of my new life, it was going to be okay after all.

Combustion

I must've dozed off right after that last glass of wine the night before. The sun was in full exposure and the city sounded like a busy stock exchange floor just outside of my window. I glanced over at my phone and discovered I had a few missed calls and two of them were from Marcus. Oh no! How could I miss our daily morning call? I had even almost overslept for my hair appointment. I glanced over at the last swallow of wine I had left behind. The cabernet had rocked me to sleep like an infant listening to its favorite lullaby. I'd needed get up out of the bed. I had so much to do to get ready for my date. My feet hit the fuzzy warm carpet that ran

Geneya Singleton

circles around my bedroom. The plush fabric made me feel like I was standing on soft pockets of air. A nice hot shower would do the job of completing my morning awakening. I'd have him sweat a little, that's it. I mean, I wouldn't want Marcus to get used to his calls being answered all the time. That definitely would not be realistic. I was honestly a busy woman. I'd just call him after I was finished in the shower.

The sweet scent of warm vanilla filled the bathroom amidst the steam from my much needed uninterrupted shower. Usually within two minutes of this serene moment, I would hear the sound of Dylan's little feet right outside of the glass doors after she had burst into the bathroom. She would typically be accompanied by her favorite teddy bear and a few headless dolls. Dylan had the idea that running water and a quiet mommy meant that it was splish-splash time for her and her plastic and furry friends. I did miss hearing her wrestle through the overfilled toy bin in her bedroom like she did every Saturday morning, but today but I was pretty sure I'd be over it soon. Today was all about me, and so far every minute of it felt so deserving. I just grabbed a simple t-shirt and some yoga pants and headed off to my day of pampering. It was just noon, so I was hoping the nail salon wouldn't be crowded like it was every Saturday afternoon. Maybe I would just get a pedicure. The process would be fairly short, and it would free me up to get my hair color touched up for tonight. I was not the best at keeping track of time so I would focus much harder today, so as not to disappoint Marcus.

Marcus! I'd almost forgotten to give him a call back. He was probably napping by now since his work shift had ended earlier this morning. Oh, what the heck, I'd call anyway. The phone was approaching its third ring

100

and just as I was about to disconnect the call when he answered.

"Well, good afternoon, sleepy head," Marcus said.

"Hello handsome!" I replied. "How did you know I was sleeping when you called?"

"Because I am pretty sure that would be your only reason for not taking my call," he said in a very firm tone. Before I could conjure up an appropriate response, he added to his unusual statement by saying, "Well that, or tending to your beautiful little girl. And since I know she is away from you today, sleeping is honestly the only acceptable reason. Oh, and death. I mean, who could really take any calls without a pulse? Am I right?"

Okay, Ava, now is the time to get the hell out of this crazy ass friendship, I thought to myself. What kind of maniac would make such a statement? Was this motherfucker planning to make me his sex slave and then murder me in cold blood? I was surely not this desperate for a damn date!

"Hey, did I lose you again, Ava?" Marcus asked as he had completely interrupted my 'victim of a serial killer' train of thought. "I was just kidding baby. You gotta loosen up around me. You're so serious and tense all of the time. Please understand that I am very humorous and loving. I would never hurt you. I promise you that."

"Okay Marcus," I responded. "You did have me concerned for a minute there. But if you are really kidding around..."

"I am, sweetheart. I promise you," he said.

"Okay, I believe you. On a serious note," I began, "I hope I didn't wake you from your sleep. I know you just

Geneya Singleton

finished your shift this morning, and I also know how important your rest is to your overall punctuality."

"Yes, beautiful, I was sleeping but I'm glad that you called. I had gotten so used to hearing your voice in the early mornings that I felt a little off track when you didn't answer. I missed you, I guess. But I am very excited about our date later this evening," he said.

"Well, that was really sweet of you to say Marcus," I said. "I, too, have gotten used to our early morning conversations and as much as I needed the rest that I've gotten, I felt a little off track myself when I awoke."

"Good. I am happy to hear that we've already created a mutual bond between us," he said. "Now what are you up to?"

"I'm out and about tying up some loose ends to get ready for tonight."

"Sounds good. I have so much in store for you tonight. I hope that you will be able to get a nap in later today to prepare for me because you will surely need as much rest and relaxation as possible."

"Is that so?" I asked. "I'm eager to see what awaits me, but I will definitely be ready no matter what."

"That's a good girl," Marcus said. "If you will please excuse Daddy while I finish my nap, I would appreciate it."

"Oh, but of course," I replied. "Enjoy your nap and I will see you later tonight."

"Okay, beautiful. Enjoy the rest of your afternoon. I will call you as soon as I awake. Goodbye," he finished.

"Goodbye," I replied.

After we ended our call, I sat in my car a few minutes to tried and catch my breath. I wondered what was really going to happen tonight between Marcus and I. I found it a bit challenging to grasp his very unique personality. I loved to live on the edge from time to time, but I would never agree to being someone's sex slave or even their homicide victim.

Oh, Ava, just get out of the car and continue on about your wonderful day, I advised myself. I had to give myself pep talks more and more these days, especially since Marcus had come aboard.

The nail salon was slightly crowded when I entered but my nail technician spotted me right away. I was a regular customer here for over ten years. I'd never needed to make an appointment with Rose during my biweekly visits. She could always spot me a mile away. She adored the bronze highlights that ran throughout my short and curly hair.

"Hi, Ava!" Rose shouted. "Come on back to my station!"

I scurried along quickly to avoid the harsh stares that were gleaming off of the faces of the other waiting customers. I could hear the muffled whispers as I walked through the small crowd.

"How are you, Ava?" Rose asked as I happily sat in her chair.

"Everything is well with me, Rose," I said. "It is so good to see you! I'm really overdue for this visit. I hate to come in when the salon is crowded like this, but tonight is really special, and I want to look my best, so I just had to come see you."

"Oh really? What's so special about tonight? And where is little miss Dylan?" Rose asked. She seemed surprised that I didn't have Dylan attached to my hip.

Geneya Singleton

"Well," I began, "Dylan is with my sister for the weekend so that I can get some much needed me time, and I also have a special date tonight."

"Oh, I didn't know you were seeing anyone," Rose replied in a very nosy tone.

"It's only been a week, but so far, so good," I said.

"Well, I'm really happy for you, Ava. You deserve so much in life, especially happiness for the beautiful heart that you have."

"Those were really kind words, Rose," I said. "I really appreciate you saying that."

"Of course! I meant every word of it!" Rose insisted.

"Okay, Rose, it's getting really thick in here and it's not the crowd."

We both broke out into laughter. I knew Rose had meant every word of what she'd said. I did deserve so much out of life and whether it be through Marcus or someone else, or even no one at all, I was truly going to begin to give myself what I had been missing for so long, and that was happiness.

Rose was one of the faster nail techs in her family-owned salon, so she would always get me in and out in a timely manner. In no time it was time to dry my freshly painted toenails. After a few more minutes of juicy salon gossip, I was ready to head to the hair salon to have my highlights touched up. I paid my bill, making sure to leave a token of my appreciation, and quickly headed out. I brushed through the crowded salon and avoided eye contact with the frustrated customers. Some were still awaiting service and they were before my arrival. I could hear the sucking of teeth from the group of irate women accompanied by the obviously annoyed stares.

Fire Without a Flame

The next stop on my list was the hair salon.

Today I was just stopping in for a color touch up and a few tight curls. I couldn't be sure what Marcus had in store for me tonight, so I decided to play it safe with the tightest curls known to man, so that if things got a little out of control between us I'd still have a little bounce left with a very vibrant color. I was a few minutes away from being done at the salon when I received a text message. It was from Marcus.

As the countdown begins, and as I think this thing through, in disbelief I sit, that my dreams have finally come true. A woman with class and unmatched beauty, who would find me so worthy to have met someone like you.

I couldn't help but smile as I read it over and over again. I didn't really know how to respond to something so simple, yet so deep. He was definitely charming and very thoughtful.

I hope this vibe lasts for as long as we do. I responded.

You have my word, young lady.

With that energy that he so smoothly sent across the airwaves, I interrupted the flow with a simple, *I can't wait to see you later.*

The feeling is oh so mutual, beautiful.

And just like that I was back on my excursion to add the final touches to my date preparations. The very last thing I would need was some of my favorite perfume. I adored the sweet, soft scent of vanilla. *Warm Vanilla Love* was the name of the signature fragrance that I would ballet-twirl in after bathing. I'd always felt that a woman should be able to stop a conversation in mid-sentence when she entered a room as she left behind trails of aromatherapy with each step.

Geneya Singleton

I was still making good time, so I decided to head to the local mall to grab a bottle. I'd seen an advertisement that the department store that carried it was running a really huge sale that weekend and I'd be a fool to miss it. I'd already reminded myself that I should go into the store, make my purchase, and head right back out. I possessed the most unforgivable habit of retail therapy. I could go into a supermarket for a dozen eggs and leave with the entire freezer section. My shopping habits for clothing and shoes were even worse. I could find fifteen different reasons why Dylan could use a new pair of shoes for each day of the week, knowing full well she would be all grown out of them within the month. I rarely purchased anything for myself once she came into my life, but she was my little doll baby and it was my God given parental right to dress her up as such.

Just like the typical Saturday afternoon busyness of any mall, parking was scarce. Finally, I spotted a woman heading to her vehicle with three small children by her side. She wore her motherly responsibilities across her round shaped face and appeared to be exhausted. The children looked to be between the ages of two and six; the youngest of them had one-thousand tears rolling down her face and was expressing her total refusal to hold firm to the woman's hand. The other two were skipping and laughing while enjoying a very delicious looking ice cream cone with rainbow sprinkles. The little one kept looking back at the path behind them leading to the mall's entrance doors. I am guessing she must've dropped her cone back there somewhere and her tears were silent pleas to mom to return back to the mall for a replacement. The mother's tolerance level with all three children appeared much better than I think I would have been able to handle.

Fire Without a Flame

I was a sucker for tears. The moment Dylan's beautiful grey eyes would present one piece of evidence of their unhappiness, I would hand over all of my credit cards with my checkbook as a bonus. I knew I had to do a better job at resisting opportunities of bribery with my little princess, but who was going to stop me? I sure wasn't anytime soon. I already had plans of filling our second garage in our mini mansion with a Mercedes Benz coupe for her to play with her Lego blocks in. Well, that was at least one of the many big imaginative things on my bucket list once I became rich and famous. I giggled to myself as I pulled into the now available parking spot that the lovely supermom had finally been able to leave me. I hoped that little fussy one would give mom a break during the car ride.

Seeing the family made me miss Dylan so much.

I wouldn't dare give her auntie a call to check in on her, as that was one of the "auntie" rules. Whenever she would take Dylan for me to get a "mommy" break, I had to promise not to harass, stalk, call, or visit during that time. Sophie was really great with caring for Dylan, so I trusted her completely. She would send daily pictures to me to confirm proof of life, as she would call it.

The department store was so neatly organized. Each window mannequin wore the most fashionable in-season outfits that screamed "buy me now!" to all the passersby and shoppers.

Stay focused, Ava! I reminded myself as I approached the doors of the department store. My eyes kept shifting back and forth between the window display and the parfum case that was situated just before the jewelry displays. My attention fixated upon what had to be the biggest and brightest diamond that sparkled under the perfect lighting in that section. I was reminded of my wedding ring that I had so graciously sold to a local jeweler after the divorce was finalized. I was pretty sure I had not gotten the total value of my ring by doing business with the town's well known corporate hijacker, also known as "Jake." I was so full of mixed emotions during that time, that I just wanted to be rid of any and all reminders of that godforsaken marriage. I was also left with the bulk of the debt that Anthony and I had accumulated, so anything of monetary value that came my way represented an opened door to the other side of torment and depression. Maybe one day I would get to do it all over again, only better than the last time.

I was warmly greeted by a friendly cashier as I approached the perfume counter. She kindly reminded me of the ongoing sale and offered me the opportunity to save cash on today's purchase by applying for their zero interest rate credit card.

I thought of the unnecessary amount of time and paper that would be involved for me to complete an application and get denied. My credit score was terrible. I wouldn't dare embarrass myself by getting declined in this very crowded department store.

"No, thank you," I respectfully declined as the young lady began to ring up my purchase.

"This perfume is one of my absolute favorites! I wear it just about every day," the cashier said as she tried to upsell me.

"Oh, is that right?" I replied and awaited her next selling point.

"Oh yes, ma'am!" she stated. I took a quick glance at her name tag. I thought it fair to know the name of the

Fire Without a Flame

person I would be saying "no" to for the second time today. "Ma'am?"

I must've drifted off again into my zone. I hadn't realized Brittany had been trying to get my attention.

"Oh, I'm sorry," I said. "No, thank you, uh, Brittany." I pretended as if I were experiencing difficulties reading her name badge. Maybe she would think I had some reading challenges and wouldn't continue to encourage me into debt.

"Okay, ma'am. Maybe next time."

"Yes, next time," I replied knowing full well if I had a "next time" with Miss Brittany, she would surely experience déjà vu.

She completed my purchase, and I was off through the crowds again. I was able to reach the entrance doors of the department store successfully before being stopped by another eager employee attempting to reach their daily sales goal. For some reason I felt as if the mall patrons were staring at me with each step I took to make my way back to my car. I was sure it was because I was displaying the biggest window of pearly whites known to man. I couldn't hold back the anxious excitement that was steadily building inside of me as the time grew nearer to my date.

Back in my car, I decided to listen to smooth jazz to calm my nerves. I wondered if Marcus was feeling as anxious as I was. He was probably more focused on my punctuality or punishment than he was on actually spending time together. I was driving a few miles over the speed limit, but I didn't care today. Adrenaline was driving me around town, and I enjoyed being the passenger. I arrived home with just an hour to spare before Marcus arrived.

Geneya Singleton

I headed straight for the shower and turned my playlist on to ease the anxiety that continued to creep in. This time I could use a little rap music. Something upbeat and hardcore. The mirrors began to fog in the bathroom. I had a really bad habit of letting the shower run while I ran back and forth between my bedroom and the bathroom completely naked after several episodes of forgetfulness. Forty minutes were left. I'll time myself in the shower today. I had a method of showering that involved intentionally losing track of time, but here was no room for that today so I'd time myself. As soon as I stepped out of the shower, I could hear a notification sound coming from my phone. Oh no! Could I have been in there longer than should I have been? Was Marcus texting me that he was outside? I gazed over at the phone as water dripped from my now frantic body.

It was Marcus, but he had not arrived. There were still thirty minutes left. He was just saying hello and how excited he was to get together soon. I replied with a simple "ditto" and a few heart-eyed emojis and continued on with my preparations. I began to apply a little foundation while recalling Marcus' request to go easy on the face beat. Something told me he would appreciate a very dark, rich and deep tone of eyeliner so I didn't hesitate to get lost with that. A nice clear coat of lip gloss and a few strokes of mascara and I was ready for the night. I sprayed two or three mists of *Warm Vanilla Love* into the air and danced in between the drops as gravity pulled them back down to me. I wanted Marcus to be distracted by my scent just as much as he would be by my body in this little number of a dress I was wearing.

Ten minutes left and I was ready to do a quick but sensual rubdown of body lotion. My skin was naturally smooth, but this body lotion that I had created by mixing a scoop of shea butter with a lightly scented essential oil was the icing on the cake. There was no way he would be able to focus much once he saw my dress and smelled the sweet aroma coming from my body. I headed downstairs to grab a glass of cabernet to calm my nerves. Marcus promised that this night would be unforgettable, and I was pretty sure he was committed to keeping his word.

The doorbell rang. It couldn't be Marcus because he didn't call first. But maybe this was a part of my punctuality and instructions adherence test.

Play it cool, Ava. Get up from the sofa, answer the door and breathe. Just breathe. It's just a date, not marriage, I warned myself. My pep talk on my way to the door only worked until I got there and looked through the peephole. I could feel my breath bouncing back from the door onto my face from the rush of nerves leaving my body. It was definitely Marcus. He stood so tall and oh so fine. His dimples were in full exposure once again. I just knew that when I opened the door, he would find a puddle of anxiety where I once stood. I hope he knew it was me.

Oh, snap out of it, Ava! It hasn't been that long since you've been on a date. Open the door and say hello, I fussed at myself. I began to slowly turn the doorknob. I could see Marcus' face light up once he realized what was happening. I pulled the door toward me and stepped forward into the remaining light of day that crept in from the moving clouds.

"Wow! You look amazing!" Marcus said.

"Thank you, sir," I replied.

"May I come in?" Marcus asked patiently.

"Oh, silly me. Where are my manners?" I asked loudly as if I had really forgotten them back inside. "Yes, please, of course. Come on in."

"I'm very pleased to see you. Especially wearing that red. Your earrings go perfectly well with your entire ensemble."

"I'm happy that you noticed," I replied.

He followed me into the living room, looking around my home as we moved towards the sofa. He smiled in approval and then, before I could turn back to offer him a seat, he grabbed my waist from behind and slightly spun me around toward him. Our eyes locked and the next thing I knew our lips were in full conversation with one another. His kiss felt so magical. His hands connected at the back of my head in such a way that I felt secure and amazed all at once. I lived the moment with him for as long as he would have me. His breath tasted like warm cinnamon bark dipped in my favorite cup of tea. Suddenly the kissing stopped. I slowly opened my eyes to find Marcus gazing through to what felt like my soul.

"Hello, beautiful," he said as if we were meeting for the first time in life.

"Hello, handsome," I replied as I struggled to regain the feeling in my lips.

"Are you ready to enjoy the evening?" he asked.

"You lead, I'll follow," I replied in a very sexy but submissive voice.

"Good girl," Marcus said.

"About that..." I said as I made an attempt to obtain an explanation for that reference.

"What about it, little girl?" Marcus asked.

Fire Without a Flame

"And that?" I added. "You see, I was curious as to know what you meant…" before I could finish my thought, I found Marcus' lips were interlocked with mine again. He paused from stealing my soul for a few seconds long enough to say, "You ask too many questions, little girl. Didn't you just say where I lead you shall follow?"

"Yes," I faintly responded.

"Then why are we still in this house? We have reservations and being late is not favorable to me."

"Yes, sir, let's go," I said.

We headed out of the house. I had never seen his vehicle before, so I was not certain which way to walk once we made it outside. I looked in Marcus' direction and waited for his signal. He walked in the direction of a very shiny, four door cherry red SUV and I followed. He stood next to me on the passenger side of the car, opened my door for me, and waited until I was completely situated in my seat and then he gently closed my door and proceeded to the driver's side. I immediately recalled my prior instructions to reach over and open his door as soon as it was time. After I completed my required task, Marcus was inside of the vehicle with me. He leaned over, offered me the softness of his lips, and when he was done, he whispered, "Good girl."

We were off to enjoy the night. He played a nice variety of R&B music that set the tone for the car ride. Marcus drove so cautiously, adhering to the speed limit across city streets the entire time. He held my hand tightly with his right hand and controlled the steering wheel with his left. Every now and then I would look up and find Marcus staring at me in total heartfelt content. We spoke a few words between us during our ride, but I wanted so badly to inquire about our destination. Instead I made small talk.

"I'm really enjoying this ride. I feel very relaxed." He smiled at me and leaned in to kiss me gently on my forehead.

"We will arrive at our destination shortly. Thank you for allowing me this opportunity to spend time with you. I trust we will do this again very soon."

"I hope so," I responded.

A few more minutes had gone by and Marcus turned off of the road and into the parking lot of a restaurant that was situated seclusively surrounded by a small lake and a few grassy hills. It appeared to be very private and peaceful. He exited the vehicle and headed for my door. He smiled as he reached for the handle, opened it slowly, reached for my hand and assisted me up from my seat.

As soon as I was out of the car, he pulled me close to him and we exchanged a very intimate kiss. This time it felt like this exchange went on for five minutes. Who cared about time when you were spending it with a man as fine as Marcus? We ended our lip locking, he grabbed my hand, and the gestured for me to follow him to the entrance of the restaurant. I had no clue where we were. I had gotten so lost in our romantic drive that I didn't pay attention to street signs or anything. It was too late now. If he was going to kill me, my stupid ass deserved to die for being a sucker for soft music and warm kisses.

"What is this place?" I asked.

"That sounds like a question," Marcus replied. "And I thought we discussed how I feel about questions." he added as he looked over to me slyly with a gentle smile.

"Yes, sir, my apologies," I said.

We had finally approached the front of the restaurant. Marcus went a few feet ahead of me to open the door and prepared room for me to enter. Once inside, I slowly gazed around to take in the scenery. There were just a few tables, soft lighting and music complimented the atmosphere. The room smelled of sandalwood and cinnamon.

We were the only patrons in the restaurant. I just figured it had been a slow night as Marcus escorted me to my seat. Our table was neatly set, and one illuminating candle and two red colored ceramic plates sat before us. The brick red napkins were professionally folded. They paired perfectly with the dinner plates. Marcus and I were seated for a few minutes and just as I was about to open my mouth to ask another question, a woman appeared from behind a beaded curtain. She had the prettiest shade of brown skin. Her hair was long, silky, and black. She wore it straight back and it bounced with each step she took toward us.

"Good evening, sir. Good evening, ma'am," she greeted.

"Good evening, young lady," Marcus replied.

"Good evening," I added. She smiled widely, showing her perfect pearl colored teeth. She brought in the scent of freshly baked dinner rolls and sweet pomegranate from the kitchen.

"My name is Allure, and I will be your waitress for the evening. May I start you both with something to drink?" she asked.

Marcus looked in my direction with the menu resting just beneath his chiseled chin as if to grant his approval for me to respond to Allure's suggestion.

"Yes, I would love a glass of cabernet," I said.

Geneya Singleton

"That's a wonderful choice, ma'am. We have a perfectly aged bottle of cabernet sauvignon that we've just added to our drink menu this evening," Allure said.

"Well I guess tonight is definitely my lucky night," I replied as I stared back in Marcus' direction who was already smiling in agreement.

He looked over at our waitress and said, "I'll have a glass of your strongest, most smooth cognac."

I felt a flutter in my stomach as he placed his order. I guess whatever was expected after dinner would most certainly be wild and memorable. Anyone that drank brown had more intent of trouble than a repeat offender preparing to be released. I just smiled at Marcus, who was now winking at me with that sexy smile emerging from behind his soft lips.

"Yes, sir, I have just the perfect drink for you," Allure said as she removed our menus and headed for the bar.

"So, what do you think so far?" Marcus asked.

"It's very beautiful and peaceful here," I replied. "I just wish I knew where I was."

"What do you mean?" he asked.

"I allowed myself to become so lost in the pleasurable ride here that I failed to pay attention to the route."

"Good," Marcus replied.

I paused for a moment as a small concern began to settle in. Where the hell was that woman with my drink? If I was going to die, I would at least like to do it with a wet palate and a slight buzz. I looked in Marcus' direction and waited for the explanation of his last statement. He was already staring back at me at this point.

"You must learn to relax and allow a man to be just that. If I wanted you be involved in the planning and execution of this wonderful evening, I certainly would have asked you to take me out on a date. Please, enjoy yourself for once and give me back my position as the pilot of this flight. I can guarantee a smooth ride with a safe landing. Do I have your word that you will not attempt to take the lead during this dinner and this relationship?"

"You have my word, sir," I said.

"Good girl," he replied.

As Marcus reached across the table for my slightly trembling hands, I could see Allure across the room finishing up our drinks behind the bar. When she made her way back to our table, she handed my drink to me first and then gave Marcus his. We thanked her and made a toast to new beginnings. Allure waited as we made our celebratory toast. She smiled and offered to take our dinner order.

"I'll have the grilled chicken salad with creamy ranch dressing and extra tomato please," I said. Just as Allure was about to confirm my order, Marcus interjected.

"You can cancel that salad, sweetheart," he said. Allure and I both looked in his direction with confusion.

"She can?" I asked.

"Yes, she will," Marcus replied. "Ms. Allure, would you please get this young lady blackened salmon over brown rice. Please add a gentle squeeze of fresh lemon juice over her salmon. Do not overcook the fish but leave it in the broiler long enough to give it a slight crispy texture. This added time will also give the lemon some zest!"

Allure looked back in my direction as if to search for approval. I was still in shock that Marcus had just taken over my meal preference, but it felt kind of sweet at the same time. I gave a quick nod and Allure understood my approval. I hadn't realized I'd been smiling the entire time even though I hadn't expected Marcus to place my order. He just winked and returned his attention to the menu.

"I'll have the shrimp scampi with extra sauce and a house salad with ranch dressing on the side. Please add extra onions and withhold the croutons." Marcus finalized his order with a special request, "Play track number 12 on the jukebox on your way to the kitchen if you will, please and thank you."

Allure walked off with our menus, food orders, and her bouncing hair. I glanced over at Marcus who was now getting up from his seat and heading towards mine. He reached for my hand and escorted me to the dance floor. The music played softly but was loud enough to create the ambiance of romance that filled the restaurant. We danced slowly with our bodies close to one another's, staring deeply into each other's eyes. Long passionate kisses were apparently on the agenda the evening because I was definitely getting my full share. We swayed to and fro with our hands interlocked at our waists. I hadn't felt this safe and peaceful in a long time, and I didn't want this night end. I rested my head on Marcus' chest in between twirls and sways. His cologne reminded me of happiness. It was a familiar smell. Maybe I had purchased it for Anthony at one point in time? The nostalgic feeling left my mind as quickly as it had entered. I wouldn't dare ruin this evening with any form of negative energy.

The song finished playing, and I felt like putty in Marcus' arms. He lifted my chin up with his index finger and situated it just at his.

"Are you enjoying yourself so far, little girl?" he asked.

"I am, sir," I replied.

"I'm happy to hear that because this is only the beginning of what's in store for you," he added.

"I'm looking forward to the rest of the evening and the rest of my life if our connection should take us that far," I said.

"Oh, we are definitely going places, sweetheart," Marcus responded.

He escorted me back to my seat and we chatted amongst ourselves while we waited for the main course to arrive; although I didn't mind having a little dessert first, and by dessert I meant chocolate, and by chocolate I meant Marcus.

Get your shit together, Ava! I thought as I attempted to pull myself back to reality. He was speaking to me, and I barely caught wind of half of what he was saying. I was too busy drifting off periodically into my own thoughts and visions of our future together. I would, of course, have to see how he was as a father to his little boy, but as a man he had already passed the test.

"Tell me about something you've always wanted to do but never had the courage to do it." Marcus randomly asked.

I had to think about that question and its answer for a few seconds. Was he trying to learn my darkest secrets? Or he is just trying to make for friendly conversation? I

didn't want to keep him waiting long.

"I've always wanted to go scuba diving," I answered.

"Really? That's pretty cool," he said. "What kept you from you from fulfilling your desires?"

119

Geneya Singleton

"I guess the fear of something going horribly wrong while I was underwater and never making it back to see my daughter grow up," I said.

"That's completely understandable," Marcus replied.

"How about you? What is something you've always wanted to do but have allowed fear to stand in the way?" I asked.

"I fear nothing but God," he replied.

I hesitated again to think of an appropriate response. Religion was a touchy subject for most, and I didn't want to unintentionally end up in church. Before I could add to my question, Marcus finished his thought. "I've done just about everything I've wanted to do in life. I vowed to myself many years ago to never live in fear but to challenge myself each day to reach new heights. I am very spontaneous, and I seek the thrills that life has to offer. The day we met, I could feel your soul calling to me. I also felt that you were going to make me work hard to earn your trust, and I respect that a lot. Moving beyond pain is one thing but living beyond betrayal is another."

He was reading me like a book. I wanted to get up and run away, but that's what I was infamous for doing. This time I decided to face my truth, even if it was coming from a total stranger. It was a breath of fresh air to have someone outside of my alter ego explain who I was.

"You are afraid and sensitive to the touch, but you will feel valuable again and you have my word on that," he promised me. I felt speechless. There was no rebuttal for the truth that Marcus had spoken.

"I'll hold you to your word," I said, and at that very moment I could see the beautiful Allure making her way back to the table with our food. Everything smelled so delicious and appeared to be smoking hot and sizzling.

"Ma'am, here is your salmon dish," Allure said as she placed my food before me. "Sir, your scampi and house salad with extra ranch dressing on the side. Please enjoy your meals, and do not hesitate to give me a call if you need me."

We both thanked her as she headed off into the kitchen again. I took a nice long sip of my wine before I began to indulge in my food. Marcus had already started eating when I looked up in his direction. He appeared to have a methodical way of enjoying his meal. He would swirl a few noodles onto his fork and once they ended in his mouth, he would sip a little of his beverage and then go right back to swirling the pasta. He made some of the sexiest sounds as he slurped each noodle off of his fork. Maybe I was just way overdue for some swirling action myself, but I did enjoy the dining show he was putting on for me.

This wine was definitely aged to perfection because it took no time to enter my system and begin loosening my thoughts and hopefully later this dress.

"How are you enjoying your meal?" Marcus asked.

"Everything is delicious, sir. I really like it here," I added. "I just can't believe it's so quiet on a Saturday evening. Talk about small business," I said.

"Oh, sweetheart, this place is typically packed every weekend. I just reserved it for the evening for just the two of us. I require your undivided attention, and I had to ensure that would be exactly what I was getting."

I just about spit my wine out as I had been in mid-gulp when Marcus made his announcement. I was speechless. I had never had a man wine and dine me so well, let alone reserve an entire restaurant.

"Wow, I can't believe you did that for me, for us," I said.

"Think nothing of it," he replied. "I really enjoy you. There will be more dates like this if you continue to be a good little girl."

My wine glass was empty by now, so the drink began to speak for itself.

"I promise to be a good girl, Daddy," I said as I gazed into his eyes.

"Very good, young lady. Very, very good," Marcus replied.

Ava! Did you just call this man Daddy? I began to speak and chastise myself internally. *Now he'll assume he has you in his corner pocket. Game over.*

I wished I could take back those words, but they were too far gone into his head. I'd just leave them there for now as a form of gratitude for this lovely evening. He'd pay me back later, I hoped. We finished our meal and sat and talked for a few hours. The conversation was so intriguing, and the chemistry was unmatched. Marcus finally signaled Allure and requested the check to be brought over.

I excused myself from the table to use the restroom. I wanted to check that my oily skin hadn't defeated my powder foundation. I stole a few selfies while I was in the restroom to post to my social media accounts since that wine had me feeling a little frisky and free. There was no guarantee that I would end the night looking as good as I did when it started. As I began to wash my hands, my phone vibrated from a notification of a text message. I could see in the subject line it was a message from Marcus.

There is a black marker just under the paper towel dispenser. I want you to write the words "daddy's little slut" just over top of your right breast and send me a picture. You have exactly two minutes to complete this task or I will come in there and assist you.

I dropped my phone on the marble sink in shock. I glanced over at the paper towel dispenser and, lo and behold, the black marker was resting there as promised. I continued to look around the restroom for a goddamn window to climb out of to get the fuck out of this place. What kind of sick bastard was I dealing with? How would he know there was a marker in the restroom unless he placed it there himself? My phone vibrated once again.

One minute left and I will enter that restroom as if I were housekeeping during check-out time.

My heart began to race, and my hands were a little shaky. *Okay, calm down, Ava, he's not psychotic or a serial killer. He has too much to lose to want to just feed a random girl like you and then murder you*, I reassured myself.

Shit! There weren't any windows in the restroom. I decided I would play along so I could make it home to see my baby girl again. I reopened the text message of instructions so I could do exactly as I was told. I felt like I was part of a hostage situation.

I removed the top of my dress so that I was down to my bra. I had no worries of anyone barging in on me since we were the only patrons tonight. I mean, Marcus had threatened to stop by, but I was already prepared for him and whatever his sexual or homicidal drive would bring. I began to write the words across my breast. I measured my writing point just below my favorite tattoo

Geneya Singleton

of a heart. I was surely a sucker for love, hence the reason why I was in this possibly life-threatening position at this very moment. The words were very much visible against my brown skin. I grabbed my phone from the sink and opened the camera app. I turned on the flash feature just in case there were any complaints from the requestor regarding clarity and visibility. Then, just like that, the photo was traveling through the communication channels between my phone and Marcus'.

I decided to wait for a response before I washed the marker off in case there was another problem to solve in this unexpected riddle. My phone slightly danced across the sink from the incoming message vibrating notification. I was a little afraid to read the message but at this point it was do or die. I opened the conversation between us.

Very good girl. Now hurry back out to Daddy.

I quickly washed the marker from my skin and redressed. I exited the restroom and headed back to my companion. Just as I approached the table, I could see Allure picking something up from the floor beneath Marcus' chair. She had a smile on her face as she walked off. Maybe he'd tipped her really well. I wouldn't be surprised, since this man appeared to be very generous and unpredictable.

"Welcome back," Marcus said as I settled down into my chair.

"It's good to be back," I replied with a slight grin across my face.

"Are you all ready to go?" Marcus asked. Was he really about to sit here and pretend as if the bathroom scene didn't occur? Now I was really confused.

"Yes, sir, I am definitely ready to leave."

Fire Without a Flame

"I've already paid the check. Let's go, little girl," he said with a sly look on that undeniably handsome face.

The bigger question was where was our next stop? In the inside of his trunk? I sure wished I had ordered another glass of wine before we left. We were back outside the restaurant and headed towards Marcus' vehicle. Some crazy part of me felt the urge to make a run for it, but the way these heels were beginning to feel deep in the archway of my foot, that just was not a feasible plan. I was a pretty good fighter, so he could dare to try me, and I'd run his entire body through the windshield of his own car.

We approached the vehicle and Marcus opened my door and then headed to the driver's seat. I guessed I should follow the previous instructions of reaching over to let him in. I did exactly as I was told during the initial trip. Once Marcus was settled in his seat, he leaned over for yet another breathtaking kiss, and I foolishly participated. This could have been the kiss of death but at least it would be a peaceful passing.

We drove for a few minutes, and I looked into the dark sky. The stars shined so brightly beyond the darkness of the night. The trees blew gently, and the air smelled so romantic. Marcus had soft music going again as we rode in silence and enjoyed one another's presence. I needed to know what fate lay ahead of me, so I interrupted the flow for a moment.

"Where are we headed?" I asked.

"Wherever you'd like, as long as I can accompany you," he replied.

Cabernet had a way of speaking to my inner spontaneity. I was torn between the next row of bushes and a local hotel. I knew should answer carefully because

Geneya Singleton

the next set of words that left my mouth would surely make the evening. Marcus' eyes continually scrolled back and forth between the road and me, awaiting an answer. I didn't feel comfortable enough to invite him over to my place for the night but at the same time, it would probably be safer for me since I knew where all of the possible weapons were kept.

"Let's go back to my place." The words exited my mouth faster than they had entered my head.

"Are you sure?" Marcus asked.

"Yes, I'm sure," I replied.

We enjoyed the duration of our ride by exchanging soft periodic kisses and hand holding. We talked about our children and their co-parents. We dabbled in past relationship conversations as well. So far there was nothing that I would take away from Marcus' charming personality. Our chemistry flowed like a reliable water source. We arrived at my home, and Marcus exited the vehicle to come and open my door for me. I reached for his hand to support my balance, thanks to my very form fitting dress, and we walked with our arms intertwined towards the front door.

My heart began to race as I could feel his warm breath swaying back and forth against the small of my neck as he still felt only inches away from my back. I fumbled for my house keys while anxiety began to encompass me. What awaited me on the other side of this door was a total mystery. I felt like a visitor in my own home. Maybe I had been taking too long to unlock the doors because Marcus gently grabbed me by the waist and announced that he had to make a run back to his car for something that he'd forgotten.

"Okay, sir, I'll keep the door open for you," I said.

Fire Without a Flame

I scurried inside to take a quick scan of the house to make sure I hadn't left anything embarrassing out for him to see. I picked up a few of Dylan's toys from the floor and ran upstairs to scan the bathroom. By the time I was done, I could hear Marcus turning the front doorknob to let himself in. I popped a fresh mint into my mouth and greeted him with my huge smile and refreshing breath as he walked in. He was carrying a small navy colored satchel of some sort. Maybe it was his murder weapon of choice. He drew nearer to me and attempted to hide the bag behind him.

"What do you have there?" I asked.

"You ask way too many questions for a woman that wants to serve me."

What the hell did he just say? I thought to myself in a repeated panic.

"I'm sorry, sir. What was that again?" I asked in a trembling voice.

"How can you properly serve me when you always want to lead?" he replied.

"What exactly do you mean by serve you?" I asked.

Before I could get an answer, Marcus reached for his satchel. I guessed now would be a good time to make a run for it to try and dodge some of the bullets from the gun he obviously had to be reaching for. Instead, I stood there squinting my eyes and praying harder than I'd ever done in my entire life. I waited in silence listening for the first bang from his weapon. A few seconds passed and still no sound. I decided to open my eyes and meet my fate face to face. As soon as my vision was restored, there this fine specimen stood gazing at me with a pair of handcuffs in hand. Just great! I'd rather have taken a bullet to leg than to be handcuffed and tortured for

127

hours or even days. It was too late for regrets now. The suspect was already in full progress in the crime.

The next thing I knew, Marcus picked me up and carried me over to the sofa. He stood me straight up at the edge of the sofa and began to lift my dress up over my head then reached for his bag once again and this time he pulled out a red satin scarf. I had no clue as to what was about to take place, but it certainly felt good. Once my dress was off from my body, Marcus placed the satin scarf around my head to cover my eyes. He then spun me around slowly two times. Once I returned to a standstill, I suddenly felt him pull my hands behind me and the cold metal from the cuffs connected with my skin like two magnets. He then turned my body toward him. I could feel his cinnamon-scented breath all over my face. Our lips locked. He came up for air long enough to whisper into my ear.

"You'll need to choose a word that you can use to express to me loudly during this session if at any time you become uncomfortable."

What the hell was Marcus talking about? Did he mean some sort of safe word? He interrupted my thoughts of concern.

"You're taking too long to respond."

Before I realized what was happening, I found myself in a downward position with my face slightly buried in the sofa. I was able to breathe freely, and I could hear out of both ears. Marcus spread my legs apart from one another and rested the palm of his hand against my bare back as to straighten my posture. He then placed that same hand beneath me and gently ran it across my torso from my rib cage down to my pelvic area. He spoke no words, but I knew for sure it meant for me to arch my back properly. He whispered into my right ear, which somehow felt that he was aware it was one of the most sensitive spots on my body. I could feel his authority being expressed with each movement.

"Your safe word is 'fire'. If at any point during this session you are unable to endure what I am about to expose you to, please utilize your word clear and loud enough that I may hear and honor your request. You do not have permission to make physical contact with my person unless given the go ahead to do so. You will abide by each set of instructions that I provide you. Additionally, if you make even just one mistake during my time with you, you will completely regret it and your mind will recall it even after tonight. Do I make myself clear, little girl?"

At this point, my heart was probably racing at a more rapid speed than any physician or God would have preferred, but there didn't appear to be an opportunity to run now.

"Yes, sir. I understand you," I replied.

"Stay here and do not move other than to breathe," Marcus instructed. He walked away from me and I could hear him fumbling through his little mystery bag again. Suddenly, I heard music playing in the background. The volume must have been at its maximum because I could no longer hear myself breathe nor could I hear Marcus moving around. I felt him standing behind me once again, only this time his skin was bare as mine. He pulled me from the sofa into an upright position and wrapped his hands around my throat. It was an aggressive embrace but felt unusually good at the same time. He leaned my body back toward his and I could feel every inch of his manhood against the crack of my ass. It was

Geneya Singleton

warm, had much girth, and I could feel the pulsation of blood flow inside of him. Moisture began to form within my vaginal walls and suddenly I could feel it slide down my legs like thick honey warmed by the sun. I had never experienced this with my own body before. I already knew I would need to be with him again, and we were just getting started.

He caressed my back and shoulders as he swayed back and forth behind me. He then removed the handcuffs from my wrists to gain better access to my backside. I could feel the tension leaving my body. It had been a while since anyone embraced my body this way. I was completely overdue for a massage and sex. Marcus must've been reading my mind along with my body.

"Stop thinking so much and enjoy my presence," he whispered into my ear. How did he know that I was heavy into thought? Did I say something aloud? "Your body is letting me know that I do not have your undivided attention. I want it all or nothing, little girl," he said. And with that, I felt a stinging sensation like no other across my buttocks.

My body buckled slightly toward the sofa. I let out a powerful scream. I also felt the warm liquid running down my thighs again. What the hell was happening here? This man was taking control of my body and my soul all at once, and I was okay with it. Another stinging sensation fell upon me. This time it was the other cheek and then simultaneously, I was being spanked and each cheek had its turn. My ass felt like shards of glass were being sprinkled upon it while being pressed to embed like tiny puzzle pieces. I began moaning and screaming repeatedly. My legs were numb, and my heart couldn't possibly still be pumping blood. The music seemed to get louder, and I could feel small whirls of wind sneak

130

past my body. Maybe I had died and was now in heaven or hell. I was caught up in a moment beyond human experience and understanding.

"Little girl, from this day forward, you will be Daddy's bitch. You belong to no other outside of myself, your biological parents, and God. You will serve me, and I will serve you. Our souls are now becoming one. Do you have any objections?" he asked.

"I do not, sir."

Just as soon as I gave my response, Marcus lifted me up and began to carry me upstairs. He moved freely about and with knowledge as if he'd explored my home prior to our meeting. He tossed me onto my bed directly on my back. I lay there completely nude and ready for more seductive behaviors.

"I'll be right back. Don't you fucking move or you will be sorry when I return," he said as he exited the bedroom.

Still blindfolded, I could hear him head back down the stairs. I was sure that he went to grab his little bag of tricks and the wireless speaker. The music grew louder, and I used the sound waves as a clue to estimate the amount of time I had remaining to regroup before being totally annihilated for the evening. He was back in the bedroom.

"Little bitch, lay on your stomach," he said as the sound of his voice grew closer to the bed.

I did just as I was told. I suddenly felt small drops of a warm fluid slowly hit my back and run down my spine. Once I was completely covered in whatever this substance was, Marcus began to massage it into my body. His hands were strong, and his strokes were full of passion. He gently turned me over on my back and

Geneya Singleton

repeated his actions on my breasts and abdominal area. His hands explored lower and lower across my body with each caress. I suddenly felt my legs separate one from the other. Marcus began dripping the warm fluids just below my navel and naturally ended up on my pelvis. Down to the lips of my vagina and the warmth of my clitoris his hands went, gently massaging up and down and around in circular motion. I moaned and squirmed all around the bed wanting to escape the plethora of emotions that were building up in me, but I also didn't want to be anywhere else in the world.

I suddenly felt his warm tongue exercising and using my clit as weights. He licked me gently and passionately. I couldn't handle much more and let out what had to be the loudest scream, which only made him lick and suck my sensitive area even harder and faster. I remembered my instructions to not make physical contact with Marcus, so I dared not grab his head to slow him down. Fluids began escaping my body more consistently, and I felt like I was going to explode. The next thing I knew, Marcus had inserted his index and middle fingers inside of me and. He thrusted them deeply in and out while licking and slurping some more. I could feel tears of relief attempting to run down the side of my face, but they could not escape the blindfold.

In and out and in and out his fingers went. I was about to lose my shit. My legs trembled and my breathing grew intense. Marcus moaned in between licking episodes. Unexpectedly, I felt a ball of spit hit me by the clitoris. It threw me off for a few seconds until he added in more fingering movements and sucking. He spit again and then sucked it right off. It felt unusually good. There was so much exchange of bodily fluids that I couldn't tell which belonged to me and what was his. The exchange was enough to trace back both of our ancestral backgrounds.

"When you feel like you are about to climax, please let me know," Marcus said.

I dared not ask why. I was certain that there was some sort of intimacy straw hiding in his bag of tricks for him to drink it all up once I was complete.

"Yes, sir," I replied.

"That's a good girl," he said, then immediately got back to business.

I wanted to remove my blindfold so badly just to see the beautiful mess that we'd made together but I didn't want to face any consequences, or did I?

Don't do it, Ava. You don't know what's lying on the other side of disobedience, I thought to myself.

Then again, who knew when the next opportunity would present itself for me to get into more trouble with Marcus? Hell, anyone for that matter. Finding a reliable sitter was least likely to work in my favor on many occasions, so I might as well live this moment out to the fullest. I began to pull back the satin scarf from over my eyelids. I had gotten it just above my eyebrows when I felt a fiery stinging sensation against my inner thigh. I looked down at Marcus whose lips and chin were glistening like a science experiment of oil and water gone wrong. It was the most beautiful sight. My love juices saturated his handsome brown skin. The air in the room was scented with scandal and sin. I wished I could bottle it up and give it away to all of the inactive bedrooms around the world.

"So, you decided to risk it all and remove your blindfold?" he asked. "Unfortunately for you, every

Geneya Singleton

incomplete thought that you allow to penetrate your mind and foolishly put into action will cause you pain." My body trembled in conjunction from the effects of his oral pleasuring of me and the suspense of what was coming next. "Did I give you permission to remove your blindfold?" Marcus asked.

"No, you did not, sir," I replied.

"Then why in the hell did you do so?"

"I had been enjoying myself so much, sir, that my anxiety would not allow me to continue to enjoy this experience in total darkness. I meant no disrespect to you at all," I finished.

"It is too late now for apologies and regret," he said. "You will suffer the consequences for your actions."

Suddenly, he aggressively sat me upright on the bed, then he pushed my body down so that my head was hanging from the opposite end of the bed. He walked around toward my head with his man stick standing erect and seemingly pointing at me. Was this man about to gag me with what appeared to be about seven inches of glory swinging from his pelvic area? I closed my eyes and kept my mouth shut for the first time the entire evening. As Marcus approached me, I reopened my eyes to ensure that he wasn't going in for the big kill. He reached for that damn bag again. I mean, it had to be a never-ending bag of tricks. He pulled out a metal looking stick. It had a tiny spiked wheel on the end of it. What the fuck was this thing? My eyes opened as wide as they could as he drew close to me with the object in hand.

"Do you know what this is, little girl?" Marcus asked.

"No, I do not, sir," I replied. In my mind I thought, *no I do not know what the hell that is and do you plan to slice up my body with it and leave me here for dead?*

134

"This is called a Wartenberg pinwheel," he said.

Looks like a murder weapon to me, I thought to myself.

"This is a sensory toy, little girl. Just relax your mind, close your eyes and stick out your tongue. Since that little mind and big mouth of yours has been getting you into lots of trouble this evening, I would like to test some things out to ensure your sensory skills are functioning properly."

Now this guy thinks he's a fucking doctor? I thought.

I decided I'd do as I was told before he reached for that bag and pulled out a machete knife. My eyes were closed, and my tongue was hanging out of my mouth like a dehydrated dog. Suddenly, I felt the cold metal of that pinwheel with its spikes rolling back and forth over my tongue. It felt a little unusual at first but then he began to massage my vagina with his other hand. While Marcus was rolling the pinwheel over my tongue, I felt a warm drizzle of fluid hit the back of my throat. It had no taste or smell. I was afraid to open my eyes to inquire for fear that I would incur yet another undesirable punishment. Another warm drop hit the back of my throat. He began to moan softly as he continued to roll the pinwheel then stopped his activity suddenly and the next thing I knew, the pinwheel was rolling gently against my breast and around my nipples. He began to kiss me on the lips until our tongues were locked together with passion and saliva. The pinwheel, surprisingly, felt pleasurable. It rolled down to my belly and headed toward my vagina. Marcus stopped kissing me, and I could hear his footsteps leave the foot of the bed where my head lay. He walked around to the center of the bed and reached for my legs then spread them apart and gently pressed down on them so that they were relaxing flat on the bed.

Geneya Singleton

He then began to rub my clitoris in a circular motion. I became so moist that his hands were slipping with each stroke. I felt the pinwheel rolling up and down my clitoris and vagina. It gave me an unusual but welcome sense of pleasure.

"You're taking this pain very well, little girl," Marcus said. I didn't quite understand what he was referring to because I felt no pain at all. "You're a masochist, baby," he added.

This intimate moment had turned into a complete learning course. He had been pulling out terminology and objects that were unfamiliar to me the entire evening.

"May I speak, sir?" I asked, as a learned lesson from a previous mistake.

"You may," Marcus replied.

"What is a masochist?" I asked.

"Someone that enjoys pain with their pleasure," he answered. Well, that pinwheel thing did not hurt one bit so maybe he was correct about that.

"Only one way to confirm," I said.

And with that, he began to run the pinwheel up and down my inner thighs and down to my ankles until he ended up at the bottom of my feet. Between the loud music and moaning from Marcus, I became partially paralyzed mentally.

Marcus had made this entire evening magical and unforgettable so far. I wished it could last forever. We went on exploring one another's levels of oddities.

"I want you to climax with me," he whispered into my ear as he lay on top of me stroking and panting heavily with evidence of his hard work dripping from his forehead.

"Yes, sir," I replied. "I can't hold on much longer, are you ready?" I asked.

"I'm ready, little girl," he replied.

His strokes grew more aggressive, and I could feel him explore my pelvic floor more deeply. The music playing in the background seemed to increase in volume. Before the intro of the next song was complete, I felt Marcus' arms begin to tremble as he dug his fists into my mattress deeper and deeper. We were moaning together in unison like we were rehearsing for a singing audition. I could feel him clamping down onto my shoulders while his thrusts grew deeper and deeper. His breathing intensified, as did mine. The music seemed to dissipate into the air as the intimacy escalated. I felt the urge to scream as I dug my fingernails into his back. I was about to lose it, but I couldn't leave Marcus behind.

"I'm ready," I said.

"Daddy is ready also, little girl."

He suddenly lifted his body from mine and then aggressively lowered himself back into me. I let out the most high pitched scream. Marcus released a deep growl. The next thing I knew, a heavy gush of warm fluids came rushing down my thighs.

"That's it little, girl! Give daddy every ounce of juices you have!"

I couldn't explain this unique response from my body. I had never experienced anything like this before. I felt like I had just signed my soul over to Marcus in red ink. After this wonderful experience, I had no intentions of breaching the contract. Marcus came a few seconds behind me. His groans were loud and masculine like the king of the African jungle. He thrusted deeply inside of me one last time and then he suddenly collapsed. Was this motherfucker dead? I had been known to be a soul snatcher in my day. I was happy to feel his heart beating through his sweaty chest against mine. The last thing I needed was to have a dead man in my bed.

We laid together in verbal silence, but the music still played in the background. Marcus came alive, looked me in the eyes, and stared for a few seconds before he decided to speak any words.

"Are you okay?" he asked.

"I feel amazing," I replied.

"Be a good little girl and go and get a warm cloth and clean me off," he demanded.

Did I look like his personal dick and balls cleaner? I mean the sex was amazing, but did this fool leave his manners at the damn restaurant?

"You're taking too long to move, little girl," he said.

Since the sex party was over, I was curious to know what he would do to me if I disobeyed the command. I sat there for a few more seconds contemplating my next move. I closed my eyes and pretended he had disappeared. Before I could reopen them, I felt a sudden firm grip on my neck. The grip grew a little tighter. Marcus sat my body upright while still holding my neck in his hands.

Oh shit, Ava! This is it now! I thought to myself. *You've really pissed him off and now you will die butt naked.* I opened my eyes wide and cautiously rehearsed breathing exercises so that I wouldn't faint.

"Listen to me you, little bitch," he said softly into my right ear. "The very, and I do mean the very, next time I give you an order, you get your sexy ass up and you get to it immediately! Do you understand me, little girl?"

Just as I was about to answer; Marcus drew his hand back and laid a gentle but firm slap across my face and then immediately kissed me in that very spot passionately. I was so confused. This experience was reality show worthy, but I wanted to stay in it at the same time.

"Yes, sir," I replied.

I hopped my happy naked ass up from that bed and ran to the bathroom as quickly as I could. I returned to find Marcus face deep in his cellphone. My jealousy kicked in immediately, and I wanted to know who he had been texting. I had to keep myself cool because it was certainly too early to ask those kinds of questions and not enough time had passed to have those kinds of "girlfriend-like" emotions. I began wiping him down with the warm cloth. From the top of his sweaty chest, to the shaft of his well-endowed penis. He never put the phone down. He even smiled while he was texting. He smiled wide and hard. I wanted to slap that damn phone from his hands so badly. How dare he explore my body in this manner all night and then entertain another woman while lying in my bed?

I headed back to the bathroom to grab a towel to dry him. I should have wrapped a few ice cubes to cool his hot ass down. I turned the music off and climbed in the bed putting some distance between us. Marcus suddenly put down his phone and my back was facing him. It was my way of letting him know I did not approve of his actions. He pulled me closer to him and held me tight, leaving a trail of small kisses on the back of my neck.

"So, did you enjoy yourself this evening?" he asked.

"Yes, I did." I replied.

"Yes, I did what?" Marcus asked as if I had forgotten to complete my sentence.

"Yes, I did enjoy myself."

I felt a slight gust of wind fly in from behind me which was then accompanied by a loud slap and a stinging sensation. Marcus had smacked me on my buttocks. I quickly reached down to rub the area and calm the burning sensation.

"Don't you dare touch it," he said.

I quickly pulled my hand back to the front of me. Marcus let out a quiet moan and began to rub the area himself. He crawled down to my back side and started kissing the area that, at this point, felt like it was on fire. He came back up my body and nudged me to turn over toward him. He passionately kissed me on the lips and spoke words in between each kiss.

"You…belong…to…me…forever," he said. "I am really connected to you in a way that I can't explain. I want to keep you in my life and very close by my side, if you'll have me?" he asked.

I wasn't sure how to process all of this. I just knew that I didn't want to see what life would be like without him at this point. I felt compelled to agree to this newly found romance. I wasn't too keen on the random physical acts of redirecting but was sure I could get used to the rewards that followed.

"I will have you, sir," I said.

With that, the next round of passionate intimacy began. We must've been at it for hours. The sun was beginning to rise, and the birds were chirping. I felt completely dry and sore in my private area. We both finally agreed to ourselves that there couldn't possibly be any more sex to be had, so we collapsed together on the bed and drifted off to sleep. A few hours went by, and I could feel movement in the bed. I had almost forgotten Marcus was there with me. For a moment I thought Dylan was home and was making her way into my bed as she would always do first thing each morning. I opened my eyes slightly to confirm that it wasn't a dream but, in fact, a beautiful reality that there was an undeniably handsome man still in my bed.

Marcus was indeed present and very much naked. He was sitting up in the bed with his back facing me. His muscles were greatly defined across his shoulders and down to his spine. I noticed where things became intense between us by the scratches I had left across his back.

"Good morning, little girl." he said. He must have sensed my reminiscing from behind him.

"Good morning, sir," I replied.

"Daddy. My name is Daddy, try again," he demanded.

"Good morning, Daddy," I said.

"Good girl, " Marcus replied. "Daddy is about to take a shower. I like my bacon slightly crispy and my eggs scrambled light. I do not like to see any brown spots from scraping the pan on my eggs. I like my coffee with cream and extra sugar. Granted, you provided Daddy with much sweetness last night; that's just the way I prefer my morning brew. Will that be alright with you?" he asked.

141

Geneya Singleton

I hesitated to respond initially. This guy was clearly cocky and crazy at the same damn time. I couldn't believe he would just open his eyes and begin making special requests and demands like he was a royal of some sort. Sarcasm formed in my head like a hangover migraine, but I could still feel the bruising from last night's bedroom marathon.

"Little girl?" Marcus said, in a tone to confirm if my ability to hear had disappeared.

"Yes, sir. I mean, Daddy. I am heading to the kitchen as soon as I get you set up for your shower."

"Good girl," he replied. Marcus headed to the bathroom, and I followed behind. I grabbed a washcloth and towel from the linen closet and demonstrated how to operate the shower. Marcus stamped his approval and expressed gratitude for my efforts by smacking me on the buttocks and sending me off to prepare his meal with a kiss. I could hear him searching on his cellphone for a music playlist to accompany his bathing time. I put on my favorite silky red robe and headed down the stairs to complete my assignment.

Since this was my first time preparing a meal for him, I wanted to make sure it was right. I pulled out the best skillets I had available. There were a few items still boxed up from mine and Anthony's housewarming. Anthony, ha! That clown couldn't hold a match to Marcus! I would use the heck out of all our gifted cookware right here and now for Marcus if he told me to.

Oh, Ava snap out of it! I quickly reminded myself.

I could hear the shower go silent and Marcus exiting the bathtub. I would have enjoyed a sneak peek of that masculine body right after a hot shower. Water drops were probably running down his chiseled chest and back.

"Little girl!" he shouted down. "Is my breakfast ready?"

I had just finished transferring his eggs from the pan onto the plate. I was taught to always make your meats first and the sides last so the sides don't go cold. I'd be damned if I would make one mistake preparing this meal for Marcus. My body couldn't handle any more consequences. The bacon was golden brown and crispy, just as he'd requested, and the eggs had not one brown spot. The coffee was richly roasted so the scent of the brew permeated the entire first floor of my home.

I could hear Marcus' feet reach the last step on the way down, so I quickly rushed his breakfast plate over to the table. He turned the corner from the stairwell into the dining room where his food awaited him. The presentation was hospitable, and I had the biggest smile on my face. Marcus reciprocated the energy, and it made me feel accomplished. He sat down at the table and began to scan his food with his eyes. I felt a little nervous but attempted to appear confident.

"Is everything to your liking, sir?" I asked.

"Indeed, little girl, indeed," he replied.

I walked off to the kitchen to retrieve his eating utensils and condiments. The coffee was steaming hot and ready to be served.

"Aren't you going to join me, little girl?" Marcus asked. "I really hate eating alone."

"I'm not really hungry," I replied.

As I returned from the kitchen with a fresh cup of coffee for him, he encouraged me to sit with him. We talked while he ate, and I enjoyed watching Marcus eat his meal. It made me feel like every bite was a short and friendly little love note of appreciation.

"Little girl, you've made me very pleased with this weekend's activities," Marcus said. "I've been single for a little while now, and I'm looking forward to changing that very soon with you if you keep this up."

Every word he spoke felt like sweet music to my ears.

"Daddy is here to stay if would like to build with me. I promise to never hurt you or show you any form of disrespect. You've sparked something in me that has awakened my soul," he added.

I could listen to him speak for hours. I just sat in awe and soaked up the romance that was spewing from Marcus' mouth. I wanted to believe every word of it, but it was just too soon.

"Why don't we enjoy the moment without making any firm commitments, if that's okay with you?" I asked.

"Little girl, your energy is unique, and your mind holds the key to my locked heart," Marcus said. "I'm not asking for your hand in marriage, but I would like an acknowledgement of what we both are feeling between us. Just tell me you will make an investment in us as I plan to," he pleaded.

"I'm here with you, sir...Daddy. Let's do what we desire and allow love to lead us to where we need to be. Agreed?" I asked.

"Agreed," Marcus replied. "Daddy must head off to get some rest before I head to work, and I'm sure you need to get to your baby girl as well," he said.

"Dylan!" I shouted. "Oh my! What time is it?" I asked Marcus.

"It's just a few minutes past noon," he replied.

Fire Without a Flame

"Yes, you are correct! Sir, I've got to get to my baby,"
I said. Sunday afternoons were "mommy and me"
activities day. "I had better get some clothes on and get
to my little princess."

"I'll see myself out," Marcus said.

"Oh no, Daddy. I do have manners," I said. "Please
allow me to walk you to the door."

Marcus gathered his things, and we walked hand in
hand to see him off to work. Once we approached the
front door, our lips immediately locked like a fierce
magnetic force. He was assertive, and I was passive
aggressive and together we made magic. After we said
our silent goodbyes, I hurried back inside to clean up
from our slumber party. Then I headed off to Sophie's
house to pick up my sweet Dylan.

As soon as I knocked on Sophie's front door, I could
hear Dylan's tiny laughter. Sophie sounded as if she was
chasing Dylan down to retrieve something she probably
shouldn't have. Dylan's little feet were taking off quickly,
like a squirrel with an acorn. All I could do was smile
because I knew that feeling oh so well when she was at
home with me. I knocked gently on Sophie's door and
rang the doorbell once. I heard Sophie inform Dylan that
Mommy was at the door and then those little feet were
on the move again as Dylan and Sophie raced to the front
door. By the drawback of the window curtain, with no
hand or face in sight, I could determine the winner.

"Mommy, mommy!" Dylan shouted as Sophie began
to open the door for me. Dylan immediately jumped into
my arms once we were face to face.

"Hi, baby!" I shouted as I embraced her. "Hi, Sophie!"
I yelled as well. Dylan clung to me as I entered the house.

Sophie hadn't realized how much she'd helped me out by keeping her favorite niece for the weekend.

"Somebody looks refreshed," Sophie said with a smirk on her face.

She grabbed me by the wrists to investigate the light bruising that appeared on each. I felt a tingling sensation run through me as I began to have flashbacks of the evening. I smiled like a Cheshire cat and continued to pretend that I was clueless to her snooping.

"Aww, come on! Spill it!" Sophie shouted.

"Well, I will say that I ended the evening in handcuffs, and it was not by law enforcement."

I intentionally walked away as the words left my mouth to keep Sophie's nose on her face where it should be and not in my business. We both giggled at the thought, and I promised to keep her up to date as things between Marcus and I progressed.

We chatted about the family and Sophie's auntie weekend. I enjoyed our sister talks. She always gave the best advice, especially about love and relationships. She never much cared for Anthony and tried to warn me that he wasn't the one for me before we were married, but I had decided to follow my heart more quickly than I did my mind. After all of the gossip topics were covered, Dylan and I packed up to go enjoy some time together. We said our goodbyes to Aunt Sophie and headed out.

Dylan's favorite activity was a toddler marathon, with her as the only runner, at our local park. She loved to discover tiny new critters and uniquely shaped rocks that were scattered about in the park. I was such a germaphobe and screeched each time she made a new discovery, especially those that could crawl or were covered in dirt. She enjoyed nature, while I enjoyed

Fire Without a Flame

flavored lip gloss and beautiful handbags. I kept a purse and car full of hand sanitizer and baby wipes to clean her up as quickly as possible.

Dylan kept me youthful and vibrant. I could run around for hours just to make her happy. She completed me. I strongly believed we were paired together in another life. The sun was beginning to set, and I knew I had to find something quick for dinner. I chased Dylan around one final time before I made the announcement that our playtime was over. She giggled so loudly when it was mommy's time to run around behind her. Her father was missing out on so much, but I couldn't make him see the things his eyes were closed to. I finally caught up with Dylan and we headed for the car. The park was just a few minutes from our home, so I didn't have much time to brainstorm a dinner plan. As we rode off into the sunset, Dylan entertained herself by admiring the people walking around the busy city streets while I mentally scanned our available meal options at home. *I'll make spaghetti!* I thought to myself. It was quick, and it was also Dylan's favorite dish.

As soon as we arrived home, I received a text message from Marcus. A huge smile immediately took over my "observant mom" face. Before I could even open the message, I began to get goose bumps all over my body, and the bruises he had left behind seemed to refresh. As I read the message, I could almost hear his voice clearly through the phone.

Hello, beautiful.

I replied with a quick response so that I could get Dylan inside and washed up for dinner.

Hello, sir.

Geneya Singleton

Dylan and I headed inside and straight to the bathroom so that I could bathe her and begin dinner preparations. I sat my phone down on the bathroom sink and got right to work scrubbing the outside world off of my baby girl. I could hear my phone vibrating and dancing across the sink. When Dylan and I were interacting nothing else mattered, so whoever it was would just have to wait until we were done. Dylan loved to splash around in any body of water. We sang and played and then bath time was over. I dressed her in her favorite pajamas and situated her in her bedroom where she could make a fun mess while mommy got dinner going.

I retrieved my phone from the bathroom sink and headed downstairs to the kitchen. As I glanced down at my phone, I could see that I had seven new text messages, and all of them were from Marcus. I panicked for a split second, hoping that there wasn't an emergency with him at work. I opened the first message.

How is the rest of your day going?

The second text read, *Hello?*

The remaining stream of messages escalated.

Little girl!

Why are you not answering daddy?

You have some major consequences coming your way.

I'm going to cause you major pain for your mistakes.

Are you okay?

I almost dropped my phone into the water I was running for the pasta. Was this man bat shit crazy? He was beginning to frighten me. Why would he send all of those messages back to back like that? These kinds of behaviors warranted a telephone call response. I picked up the phone and began to dial his number. As the phone rang, my heart rate increased. What the heck had I gotten myself into? This guy was clearly looney. I'd never met a man who wanted to keep tabs on me and definitely not one that was so clingy and aggressive at the same time.

"Hello, beautiful," Marcus greeted.

"Hi, are you alright?" I asked with great concern.

"Yes, I am. Why do you ask?" he responded as if nothing had occurred between us.

"Well, I am asking because of the multiple messages you sent to me in such a short period of time," I said. "Even if I had been in a position to answer you, you certainly did not leave much time in between messages to do so. I was taking care of my daughter, and when I am doing so I will never utilize my phone or engage in anything that will take time from her."

"I understand, little girl. Daddy is really sorry for overreacting, I thought you may have been doing something that would have made me displeased with you," he said.

"What would that be?" I asked him while in my mind thinking how strangely he was behaving, especially at this early stage in our friendship. However, a small part of me enjoyed feeling valued for once. If one night with Marcus had him feeling this way, I could only imagine how things would be months down the line. I would surely become Mrs. Marcus before winter had set in. "What crossed your mind when I had not responded to you?" I asked him.

"Daddy thought that he may have been too rough with you last night and maybe you were making your exit," he replied.

"No, I'm here Marcus, but I will never take any time or attention away from my daughter so we must work together on respecting this space," I informed him.

"You have Daddy's word that this will never happen again."

"Okay," I reluctantly agreed. Somehow, I knew this would not be the last time he would behave this way. "Anyway, how is your work shift going?" I asked to switch up the tempo of this slightly uncomfortable conversation.

"Everything is really quiet here. The city must be asleep, and I'm okay with that." We both giggled at the remark.

"Well, I hope it stays that way for you guys," I said. "I will have to give you a call back a little later after my daughter and I finish our dinner and she is in bed. Will that be okay?" I asked sarcastically.

"Indeed, beautiful," Marcus replied.

"Okay, Daddy, I will talk to you later," I said and disconnected the call.

I headed upstairs to check in on Dylan and assess the damage at toddler headquarters. Dinner was ready to be served so I walked into her bedroom and scooped her up.

""Time to eat, Mommy?"

"Yes, baby. Let's go."

Dylan and I headed down the stairs to the set dinner table. She'd started joining me at the big table just a few months ago. She was always excited to sit with me instead of at her toddler dinette set. Her feet dangled from the wooden chair so freely, and she preferred to sit at the head of the table like she was the queen of this castle. We talked about the week ahead and all of the fun activities that awaited her at daycare with her teachers and classmates. They had a field trip planned to go see a children's musical at our local theater, and she was really excited about that. She loved to sing along and dance to all kinds of music. She was so much like me in that way. Just a kind, free spirit enjoying the simple pleasures of life.

We finished up our dinner and cleaned up our mess. Little Miss Spaghetti Face found the most humor in seeing mommy play "pickup" with the millions of pasta noodles that were decorating the floor just beneath her place at the dinner table. After we were all cleaned up, we headed for the family room to watch a movie before bedtime. Dylan's favorite movie was Cinderella. We've watched it more times than I can even remember.

"Derella, Mommy!" Dylan shouted as I turned on the television.

"Yes, baby, we are going to watch Cinderella."

For the millionth time, I thought to myself. She began to clap her hands in excitement then pulled her favorite blanket from the sofa and headed to her movie watching spot in the middle of the floor. I sat down next to her and we watched and sang along for the entire show. Before the movie was over, Dylan was sound asleep in my arms. I carried her up to her room and tucked her in tightly. I prayed that tonight was the night she remained in the "big girl room" throughout the night. She would always awaken in the wee hours of the night and come to my bedroom to climb in bed with me. I didn't mind it much since it was just she and I, but if Marcus turned out to not be a serial killer, we would have to work on this a little harder since he would be living with us. I chuckled at the premature thought. It was fun to fantasize about not being a single woman as well as a single mother.

Speaking of Marcus, I thought I'd better go and find my phone so I could check in before he flipped out again. When I reached for my phone, I was very much surprised that there were no messages from him. Maybe he'd heard my request for space loud and clear. I decided to send him a nude photo just to shake things up a little. I was definitely bold, but he made me feel more confident. I pressed send, and then a slight pang of regret filled me suddenly but there was no turning back. The photo was off to Marcus. An immediate reply came through from him,

You sexy little bitch. You made Daddy's night. I can't wait to see you again.

I smiled at the confirmation that he was pleased with my actions.

Likewise, Daddy. I replied.

We texted explicit photos and X-rated conversations for the next few hours. It was getting late, so I excused myself from the fun so that I could get a good night's rest. Marcus agreed and we ended our phone sexting happily.

The next day Dylan and I awoke to our daily routine of preparing for work and daycare. As we headed out of the door, I looked up at a tall shadow hanging out by my car. I had to do a double take to ensure my eyes were not deceiving me. Surely as the day was new, there stood Marcus waiting by the passenger side door. My heart began to race with various combinations of emotion. Why was his crazy ass waiting for me outside of my home and who authorized this visit? I didn't know if I should run back inside, lock the doors, and call the police, or land a solid punch across his now not so fine face. Dylan was with me so I didn't want to make any sudden moves that would startle her. I also did not want to make a scene outdoors.

"Marcus?" I said in a very confused and uncomfortable tone.

"Good morning, beautiful," he said so calmly, as if he were a resident in the neighborhood and had every right to be here right now.

"What are you doing here?" I asked.

"I just wanted to say good morning in person. I hope that's okay?"

"Mommy?" Dylan said, as to see if everything was alright with me and this unwelcomed. "Fireman," she said as she pointed to Marcus, who was still in full uniform.

We both stared at Dylan in shock that she either remembered him from our first meeting or she could identify his profession by what he was wearing. Both ideas were surprising for someone Dylan's age. She broke the tension between us for the time being. After I buckled Dylan into her car seat, I walked around the vehicle to come face to face with Marcus.

"Why would you just show up at my home unannounced?" I asked, now frustrated again.

"I'm sorry. You were on my mind all night, and I just had to see you," he pleaded.

"Marcus..." I began to speak but was suddenly interrupted.

"Daddy. My name is Daddy, little girl," he said.

"Listen, Daddy, if this thing is going to work between us, you must learn to respect my space. You can't just

Geneya Singleton

show up at my home unannounced and certainly not while my daughter is at home," I said. "Between the impatient text message responses from you last night and this pop-up visit, you're starting to make me very uncomfortable."

"I'm sorry, little girl. Daddy meant no harm. This will not happen again, I promise," he said.

"I will speak with you later. I need to get to work." I dismissed Marcus and the entire conversation, entered my vehicle and drove off. I watched in the rearview mirror to ensure that the crazy son of a bitch was not following me. I felt pretty nervous but kept my cool so that I did not frighten Dylan. We arrived at the daycare, and I dropped her off. In my mind I wondered if I had put our lives in danger by entertaining Marcus. I needed to calm my nerves as soon as possible. If anyone could help me make sense of this, it would be Salene. I gave her a quick call before I arrived at work.

"Hey girl!" she answered excitedly, as always.

"Salene!" I shouted.

"What's the matter?" she asked.

"You know the firefighter…well, Marcus and I had our first date over the weekend, right?"

"Yes!" she said, waiting for me to spill the tea.

"Well, he reserved a small restaurant for us," I started.

"Oh, you mean he made reservations for the both of you?" she asked.

"No, girl. He made private reservations with the restaurant so that we were the only patrons."

"Oh, how beautiful! He sounds like a keeper!" she said.

"Wait, there is more," I said. "He ordered me to do kinky things and send him pictures while I used the restroom at the restaurant."

"Okay, that doesn't sound stressful," she said.

"No, that wasn't bad at all, but after dinner we took a nice romantic drive to my house, then had wild and passionate sex all night."

"That sounds hot!" Salene said.

"Yes, he used all kinds of sex toys and strong hands to please me."

"Hell, I'm getting worked up just listening for the problem."

"Well, this morning he showed up at my house unannounced. When Dylan and I walked outside to get in the car, he was standing there like he was a valet or something," I said.

"Are you freaking kidding me?" Salene shouted.

"I was terrified!" I said.

"I am sure you were, as anyone would be."

"I asked him why he would just show up to my home, and he said I had been on his mind all night and he just had to see me. I told him to never violate my personal space again if he wanted our friendship to continue. He promised me that it wouldn't happen again, and I left. What do you think I should do?" I asked Salene.

"Do you believe that he has learned from his mistake?" Salene asked.

"He seemed sincere when we spoke. I guess I don't have a reason not to believe him," I said.

"He didn't follow you or put up a fight to go against your request, did he?" she asked.

"No, he didn't," I replied.

"I say give him another chance. If he shows just one small clue that he needs to be on medication, run like hell and never look back," she said. We both burst into laughter at the idea.

"Okay, Salene, I'll go with your advice, but if he so much as breathes one too many times, I'll cut off his privates and mail them to his mother." Salene laughed even louder this time. She knew my sense of humor was unique and at times psychotic. "I'm pulling up to work now, girl. I'll call you later. Thanks for the talk," I said.

"Keep me posted," she requested.

"Will do, bye."

We ended our call and I headed into work. I hoped the day would be less exciting than my morning was. Halfway through the day I received a text message from Marcus.

I hope you are having a great day. I'm sorry again for just showing up at your house this morning, and I hope you can forgive me.

I had to take a few minutes to decide how I would respond and if I would respond at all. I really enjoyed spending time with him, and I was very impressed with the chemistry we shared. I believed that he was remorseful about his actions, so I decided I would keep him around.

Hello, Daddy. My day is going very well. I replied.

Daddy is just resting from his long work shift and thinking about you. I appreciate you giving me a second chance and I will make up for my mistake.

We will be okay. I assured him.

Fire Without a Flame

That's what Daddy likes to hear. Do you have any writing utensils nearby? he asked

I do have a few ink pens, a highlighter, and a marker, why do you ask?

Please take that marker and excuse yourself to the restroom and do something to make Daddy smile.

I couldn't believe he was up to these antics again. I hesitated to obey his instructions but then I recalled the reward that had come with my obedience the other day. I could definitely stand to cash in some "daddy credits."

Yes, sir. I replied and grabbed the most permanent of markers then headed for the rest room.

I checked to ensure I was all clear by scanning the area. I scurried off into the first stall and got to work. I drew three hearts with arrows that pointed to my right breast. Just beneath that I wrote out "Daddy's little slut." The fumes from the marker were breathtaking but so was the spanking that awaited me if I disobeyed. I snapped a quick photo of the artwork and sent it in a text message to Marcus. I began to wash off the evidence in the restroom sink and awaited his response. Before the brown paper towel could absorb the faucet water from my smooth skin, my phone vibrated across the sink's countertop. Marcus had responded.

You are quite the obedient one. Daddy wants to lay you across his lap and spank you until your beautiful brown skin is a fair shade of maroon. I love to leave beauty marks all across your body as proof of ownership.

Ownership? I replied. This guy was moving faster than the speed of lightning but I guess I was down for the ride.

Yes, you belong to Daddy now. he told me.

Geneya Singleton

I wasn't sure how to respond or even what he meant by that statement, but it had been a while since anyone had claimed ownership or so much as provided me with this kind of attention. I decided I would go with the flow of things.

Okay, Daddy. I'm yours for the keeping.

I may have just signed my soul over to the devil but when you've already been through hell, there isn't a flame hot enough to burn.

Good girl. You will not regret this day for as long as you live. You have daddy's word on that, he replied.

I wasn't exactly sure about what this meant for us. I hope I didn't just sign a lease for infinite unannounced pop-ups to my home and workplace or even Dylan's daycare.

Snap out of it, Ava! He knows better than that, I thought to myself. *Just enjoy the ride. You can make an exit anytime you're ready.*

We texted half of my shift. My face lit up like a decked hall of Christmas lights. My colleagues could feel my newfound energy and made comments throughout the day. I couldn't have cared less about what anyone thought of me. I was finally happy again and intended to take it all in one day at a time.

The Bonfire

Twelve months had gone by and, Marcus and I were so involved in one another's lives. Our children were close like twins separated at birth. We spent quality time together as a couple and as a family. The spankings were frequent and still oh so rewarding. I hadn't had much time for family and friends. Marcus liked for me to stay close to him. He allowed me to visit a few friends from time to time but no overnight stays. I was required to share my GPS location in real time through an app he installed on my cell phone each time I traveled anywhere. He said it was for my protection and his peace of mind for him to be aware of my whereabouts at all times. I also had to send detailed proof of my environment when I was away from him. He required me to send photographs of everyone in my presence wherever I was. He said it wasn't that he didn't take my word as truth, but more so that it made him feel like he was with me when I was on the go.

The new life that Marcus introduced me to was very unique and thrilling. Our sexual lifestyle was called B.D.S.M., a form of domination that wasn't for the weak or faint of heart. Marcus was the dominant one or "dom", and I was the subordinate or "sub". I referred to him as "Daddy" at all times, unless we are around people that we did not care to share our private affairs with. Many wouldn't be able to understand it anyway. The few friends that I had shared my secret with felt as though Marcus was holding me in some sort of emotional prison. They didn't understand why I hadn't had much time to talk and visit with them anymore. Most people in relationships shouldn't have a lot of spare time to hang out with their single friends, or so I thought. It was fine by me if they judged something that they didn't know much about. I didn't mind it much at all. The way my life was presently, I felt like I was on a natural high and I didn't want to come down. Having to check in with Marcus each time I made a move reassured me that if I were in any kind of trouble, I would have the security that someone would be watching over me and that help wouldn't be but a "Daddy check-in" away.

I could hear the sounds of the busy city streets in motion through the cracked window. I was ironing Marcus' work uniforms for the week. He liked his uniforms freshly pressed, neatly resting on a hanger and at his disposal. He kept a few at my house for when he visited overnight. The breeze creeping in from outdoors felt so cool gliding across my melanin skin. I kept watch for the window curtains that they did not blow too hard from the whispering wind. Marcus required me to remain topless whenever I ironed his clothing, and I wouldn't want to become exposed to the world outside. I would be highly embarrassed if the curtains had blown open and the neighbors caught a glimpse of my bare skin. As frisky as I'd become, it might not be such a dreadful thought after all. I giggled at the thought of dear old Mr. Frank, my neighbor. He was approaching the wise age of seventy and his poor little heart would probably stop ticking if he bore witness to these fun bags' as Marcus called them.

Marcus required me to send photo and video proof whenever I was ironing in his absence. So, I had to abide by the rules. This weekend coming is our one year anniversary and Marcus told me that we would be going away on a surprise vacation. The details of our trip were not made known to me. He instructed me to pack really light and specified that some adult toys and a few pairs of panties were all that I would be needing. He said I wouldn't be wearing much of anything the entire vacation. This sounded like my kind of getaway. Marcus knew exactly how to keep the flames burning in our relationship. This would be my first time away from Dylan in a very long time. Although it would only be for a few short days, I was still a little uneasy about leaving her behind. I rested in the assurance that she would be in good hands with her favorite aunt, Sophie, like always. I needed to take a quick trip to the mall to grab a few things for our vacation. Dylan was on a visit with

Anthony, so I decided to make a run for it while I had the free time.

I sent a text message to Marcus asking for approval to leave the house. Because of his unpredictable work and sleep schedule, he had previously permitted me to make unapproved moves if he did not respond within a certain time of my request. Ten minutes was the window. He had not responded so off I went to the mall. I wanted to surprise him with a gift for our anniversary, and I knew just the store to find it in. Marcus was a huge sports fan and there was a store in the mall that customized all kinds of sports memorabilia. He loved to wear hats, especially those that he could represent his favorite team with. I wanted to get him a baseball cap with his favorite football team's logo and would have them stitch our initials and anniversary date underneath the brim. I was too excited to contain the surprise, but I dared not let the cat out of the bag. Marcus could easily persuade me to do whatever he said naturally, so if I had even mentioned one clue about a surprise for him, I would end up telling it all. He just had a way with words that made me melt.

I arrived at the mall and was pleased to find several available parking spots. This meant that I should be able to run in the mall and back home before Marcus awoke, so there was no need to share my geographic location with him at this point. I headed inside of the mall and my first stop was to my favorite department store for a bottle of *Warm Vanilla Love* perfume. I would need a fresh bottle for our trip. After my purchase there, I was off to the sports memorabilia store to place my custom order. The order would take about a half hour to fulfill so I killed time in the lingerie department of a store nearby. I needed a few numbers to keep Marcus busy for the entire vacation. Of course, each sexy piece had to come in the color red if I wanted to return home with a few bruises or as I called them Daddy's custom made souvenirs. Chills passed through my body just envisioning the good times we would have on this trip.

I approached two of the most breathtaking pieces of lingerie. They screamed Daddy. I made my purchase and left to check on the status of Marcus' gift. All of this running around made me work up an appetite, so I decided to stop at the food court to grab a bite to eat. There were quite a few patrons sitting around chatting and scarfing down delicious meals. I had a taste for a good 'ole burger and some french fries, so I proceeded to the counter to place my order then I decided to sit and enjoy my meal since I didn't have to rush back home for anything. I was so grateful that Dylan was finally getting to spend time with her father. He was stepping up to the plate more often these days, especially since Marcus had come into our lives. Anthony felt intimidated that another man was around and performing some of his duties as a father.

As I enjoyed the savory flavor of my juicy burger, I scanned the food court in admiration of the joyous faces around me. There were little children happy to be out and about with their parents and couples sharing romantic bites of dishes. Life seemed to be working in favor of us all. I reached for my cell phone in my purse to check for any calls from Anthony or Marcus. Nothing from either. I felt so peaceful. Marcus must've really been tired after his shift last night. He would have normally gotten up by now to grab a drink of water or make a bathroom run. Oh well, I would let him rest. We had a busy weekend coming up, and he would definitely need all of his energy.

After I finished my meal, I headed back to the store to pick up Marcus' anniversary gift. As I approached the business, I caught a glimpse of a man and woman walking in the opposite direction. I must have been really exhausted from my errands because I thought the man resembled Marcus. He was of the same height and build. It was kind of hard to see clearly because the couple was walking hand to hand and very close together.

Oh, get it together, Ava! I said to myself.

That couldn't be Marcus. He was at home fast asleep, and besides that gentleman was with a woman and I was the only woman aside from Marcus' mother that would ever be walking that close to him. The couple moved swiftly about the mall. They stopped for a second to share a long kiss between them. The moment they turned to face one another, glass shattered on the floor of the food court. My heart stopped beating and the scent of my favorite perfume filled the surrounding air. I had dropped my shopping bags and felt a dizzy spell come upon me suddenly.

People were staring in my direction, and I could do nothing but stand there. My lips felt dry and my tongue became stuck to the roof of my mouth from the onset of lethargy. It was Marcus in the flesh, and he was kissing another woman. She had short blonde hair and stood about five foot six. She was of a caramel complexion and her body had a slim build. She had her hands wrapped tightly around my man's head as she enjoyed their passionate kissing. I couldn't believe what I was witnessing. The betrayal hit me like a ton of bricks. I had to move away from the staring crowd and the mess I had made from the broken perfume bottle.

Everything in me told me to approach the two of them but I knew my temper was too unstable to resist imprisonment. I ran off to find the nearest restroom to dry my tears and regain my composure. I had so many questions running through my mind. How could he have done this to me? It felt like my failed marriage all over again. My heart was racing at a rapid pace. My palms were sweaty, and my eyes were full of tears and enragement. I couldn't call anyone to help calm me because I was too embarrassed to even discuss this type of betrayal and heartbreak. I especially wouldn't let my best friend Salene know a word about any of this.

I cleaned my face up and left the mall. Once I got to my car, I broke down again. I never saw any of this coming. Marcus and I were so close and so happy with one another, or at least I thought we were. Once again, I was blindsided by love. But this time I would strike back. I decided not to say a word to Marcus about what I had witnessed. If he loved me the way he'd expressed, both physically and emotionally, he would come clean on his own. I headed back home and awaited Dylan's return and hopefully a phone call confession from Marcus' cheating ass.

Inferno

Three hours later and still no call from Marcus. Dylan was back home and sound asleep. The evening grew longer and still no calls or messages from Marcus. I decided to give him a call just to see if he would answer. Four rings in and straight to voicemail. My fury brewed inside of me. All kinds of thoughts festered in my mind. If Dylan hadn't been home, I would have hopped in my car and paid the two love birds a visit. I poured myself a glass of wine and put on some soft jazz to help calm me. I paced the floors and cleaned every area of the house where I could find dirt. I even polished

Geneya Singleton

the silverware three times. No Marcus all night. I needed to get some rest because I had work in the morning.

The sun was out and there were sounds of birds chirping. I reached for my cell phone to check the time and see if Marcus had come back from his disappearance act. There were no calls and no messages to see. Thanks to that third glass of chardonnay the night before, I'd overslept by forty-five minutes.

"Shit! We are really late!" I shouted.

I could hear Dylan's footsteps heading into the bathroom just down the hall. I hopped out of my bed and hurried to meet her. She was such a big girl, so independent. I greeted her with a smile and a happy dance. She laughed at her silly mommy and got back to her business.

"We overslept baby!" I said to Dylan.

"Late mommy?" she asked.

She was so intelligent. She knew exactly what was going on. We hurried to get ready to get out of the house and begin our day. During my drive to the daycare I waited impatiently for the phone to ring. I just knew Marcus would have a ball of common sense knock him in the head at full speed at some point, but maybe not. Maybe he was still in bed enjoying his little shopaholic whore. I hated his guts so much! I dropped Dylan off at her daycare and headed into work.

I sat in the parking lot for an additional few minutes to let out one final cry and fix my makeup. No one would see me break a sweat. I had bragged so much about my relationship that I wouldn't dare let anyone know I had allowed someone to break me once again. The day went on and I'd successfully hid behind my mask of happiness.

Just as my work shift ended, I received a message from the infamous cheating bastard.

Hello, beautiful.

It took everything in me to not lose my cool and let him have it. I promised myself I would keep things together at least until we returned from vacation. He could fuck up all he wanted to but he was for damn sure not going to ruin my first kid-free get away in what had felt like forever. He was going to spend every dime in both his pockets and his pension when I was through with him. I wanted so much to let him know that I'd witnessed his sorry ass in the mall with that whore, but I had two more days to play things off.

Hello Daddy. I replied.

Daddy is sorry he took so long to contact you. My phone was broken after I accidentally dropped it in a bucket of water while cleaning the house yesterday. I had to wait for it to dry out before I was able to use it again.

Okay, Daddy. A bold faced lie deserved no more from me than a short answer.

How are you feeling today, little girl? he asked.

I am well, Daddy.

Daddy is so looking forward to spending those magical days away with you for our anniversary. I have so much in store for us.

I bet. I replied.

Excuse me little girl?

I'm sorry, Daddy. I meant I am looking forward to it as well. I replied, lying through my teeth.

Daddy will meet you at your house after work.

Okay, Daddy.

Geneya Singleton

I hoped I had a fresh bottle of bleach that I could replace his drinking water with at the house. Maybe then he would come clean.

Later that evening, after Dylan and I had eaten dinner and she was off to bed, I could hear keys turning at the front door. Certainly, it had to be Marcus. I sat on the sofa in anticipation. Maybe I would throw something in his direction that would hopefully hit him in the eye or in the forehead. It might be easier to grab a knife from the kitchen and stab him repeatedly. Today he would learn the position of a subordinate. I wanted to dominate him like the little bitch he was. Betrayal hurt more than a stab wound surely, so I decided to keep my cool. The color returned to the palms of my hands as I released the tight fists I had been clenching the minute I'd felt his presence.

"Hey, little girl," he said as he entered my home.

Be cool, Ava. I coached myself silently.

"Hi, Daddy,"

I replied. He walked towards me and landed those lips that were smothered in infidelity on my forehead as he'd always done when he greeted me, then began to make small talk about the day behind us. I participated cordially so as not to let him in on the scornful revenge I was plotting. Marcus' best friend Timothy had always had eyes for me. He flirted often. Maybe I would finally give in to his advances and record him and I having hot steamy sex, then send a copy of the betrayal to Marcus. Oh, who was I kidding? I was not that kind of woman. I just wanted to hurt him the way that he'd hurt me.

"Something is off with you, little girl. Come sit on Daddy's lap and tell me what's going on. Your energy is completely off." I sat in hesitation and obvious

Fire Without a Flame

frustration for a few minutes. My body felt so numb,
almost paralyzed. "Little girl, bring your ass over to
Daddy now!" he shouted.

I slowly approached him and challenged him to a stare
down. I wanted Marcus to see the pain in my eyes for the
last time. I was going to leave his sorry ass just as soon
as we returned from our vacation. I stood before him,
lifeless. Maybe the color had left my eyes and all that was
left were two black holes that led straight to my soul. He
needed to see that all of the feelings that I once held for
him were long gone.

"What's going on with you, little girl?" I had no
answers available. I held back the tears behind my
eyelids. Revenge was best served cold, so my plans to
annihilate Marcus' manhood would feel so much better
after my all expenses paid vacation.

"Everything is okay, Daddy," I replied.

"Then get upstairs, remove your clothing, and stand
in the corner. If you want to be dishonest with me, you
will think twice about ever doing it again," he said.

I was in no mood for anything remotely kinky but
between my broken heart and need to cry, what would
be better than a beating from Daddy. I headed to my
bedroom and removed every last article of clothing as I
had been instructed. I faced the wall just beside the bed.
Marcus entered the bedroom and closed the door behind
him. He then reached for his cellphone and began to
search his music playlist. There was a special list that he
played when I was in big trouble. The songs were full of
explicit lyrics and heavy instruments that produced
sounds that could muffle any loud screams. He was
mindful of Dylan being asleep in her bedroom just down
the hall, so he kept the volume at a fair level and I would

Geneya Singleton

have to do the same. He approached me from behind, and I could feel cold metal gliding up and down my spine. This time he pressed a little harder to make me aware of his disappointment in my dishonesty. Marcus could always see right through me. I could only wonder, if we were so mentally connected, why would he not think that I would realize his acts of infidelity? Even if I had not witnessed it with my own two eyes, we were of one soul and eventually his darkness would become exposed to the light. The spikes were much colder this night, surely because of the distance between us.

I wanted to grab that pinwheel and run it across his penis until the floors were covered in his unfaithful DNA. I gave little response to his sexual advances. How could I be turned on by this monster? I felt the pinwheel gliding across the back of my neck and then, suddenly, it stopped. Marcus pressed harder and harder until I could feel a slight burning sensation.

"If you want to keep secrets from Daddy, you will suffer in silence. Don't you let out one fucking sound, do you understand me?"

My skin had broken, and blood began to run down my back. The pinwheel hit the floor. The next thing I knew, I was on my hands and knees on the floor. I could hear him struggling to undo his pants and belt buckle. A whipping sound filled the air as he began spanking me with his belt. A quarter inch thick leather strap met my back and legs repeatedly for ten minutes. The pain felt like heaven. I never made a sound. I welcomed every lashing like a good girl. My legs began to stiffen, and the welts were hot like a slow volcanic eruption. This was exactly what I needed to regain my strength and flawlessly execute my plans for revenge on this son of a bitch.

Fire Without a Flame

When we finished making love, Marcus fell fast asleep. I cleaned our mess and iced my wounds. The emblem from his firefighter belt buckle was embedded across my thighs like three dimensional tattoos. I climbed into bed next to him and enjoyed the leftover scent of disobedience that filled the room. I looked over to the nightstand and realized Marcus' phone was sitting there unattended. Surely there would be some evidence in his phone about his newfound lover from the mall. I quietly crept out of bed and reached for the phone, heading straight for the text messages and call logs. I peeked over to ensure that he was fast asleep before I began my investigations. Marcus was snoring loudly, and his eyes were closed tight.

A few messages in, I came across a name and number that I didn't recognize. Marcus and I knew all of each other's family and friends so surely this had to be her. The name read as "Star." What kind of name was that for a woman? Maybe she was some sort of exotic dancer. There were a few interesting messages between the two of them and quite often. My heart stopped as I reviewed some messages where she referred to him as Daddy. The conversation thread went as far back as six months ago. They had been sharing explicit photos and X-rated conversations. I could see her face so clearly, and it was definitely the girl from the mall. I wanted to die in that moment as I scrolled further through. There were even a few pictures of her in Marcus' bedroom. Tears began to fill my eyes and my heart raced rapidly. The truth was finally out in the open and a part of me wished that I had not known any of this. I dried my tears and climbed into bed. I decided to pretend just for a few more days that none of this had occurred. I lay lifelessly besides Marcus.

We both were cold to the touch. His heart and my desire for him had left the bedroom and this relationship.

Morning came and I jumped right into my routine of getting us all ready for the day while Dylan was still sleeping. That beating the night before had made a huge impact on my attitude. Nothing but artificial smiles and fictitious joy. Marcus had no clue what was in store for him. He enjoyed the morning view of my domestic duties: me, ironing his uniform while topless. I knew how to follow a script like a well-seasoned actress. I prepared his breakfast to go and saw him off to work.

"You make Daddy so happy," he said with a kiss to my forehead and then he vanished off into the dawning day.

It felt like the Judas kiss of betrayal, but I accepted it with honor. Tomorrow was our anniversary and departure to wherever he had in store for us. I'd just remembered I'd never gotten a chance to pick up Marcus' gift from the sports memorabilia shop. I had been so sidetracked at the sight of Marcus and pole dancing Star swapping saliva and holding hands. Oh well, he didn't deserve a gift anyway. I transitioned back to reality and proceeded on to my motherly duties.

It was my time together with Dylan and nothing would ever interfere with these joyous moments, not even the pain that Marcus had brought into this house. I headed for Dylan's room to awaken her and, to my surprise, she was waiting by the stairs for me with a huge smile on her beautiful face. Immediately all hurt and worry left me.

"Good morning, baby!" I shouted.

"Good morning, Mommy! Marcus go to work?" she asked.

Fire Without a Flame

"Yes, baby, he did," I replied. She loved Marcus as her own father. It was going to be really tough explaining to her why he would no longer be a part of our lives. He had been the only stable father figure she'd experienced. I even considered pretending none of this had happened, to continue living this lie, but I realized that living unhappily just to satisfy a heart's desire would ultimately become more toxic than a drug addiction. Marcus was my addiction and he satisfied every craving for a hit. How could a person want to become free from something that had made them feel so alive?

"Mommy?" Dylan said with an expression to question if I was still present.

"Sorry, baby. Let's get ready for the day."

We showered and dressed, then enjoyed a quick bite of her favorite chocolate chip pancakes with some mixed fruit. I got through the workday peacefully. Marcus stayed in contact for a great deal of the day. After work I picked Dylan up from daycare and dropped her off with Sophie. Marcus and I were leaving tomorrow for our trip. I avoided spending too much time with Sophie today in fear that she would detect my pain and pull the truth out of me. I provided her instructions to care for Dylan for the next few days and then said my goodbyes.

I made it home just as the sun was setting. When I entered my home, I found a lovely surprise awaiting me on the kitchen table. There was a bouquet of flowers and balloons. "Happy anniversary to the love of my life," read the enclosed card. I smiled at the gesture. He had gotten a dozen of my favorite flowers. A few hibiscuses mixed with red roses. They smelled so sweet and fresh. He was always such a gentleman and very thoughtful. If only he had thought of me when he crossed paths with

Geneya Singleton

that whore. I bundled the bouquet together and tossed them in the trash can. If he thought that some cheap flowers was going to cool the burn, he was sadly mistaken.

Thank you for the flowers, Daddy. I texted him.

Anything for my beautiful girl. Daddy will see you first thing in the morning when we leave for the most romantic and memorable vacation you will ever experience.

"Okay, motherfucker," I said aloud, but replied with a few heart shaped emojis.

I was getting pretty good at pretending that Marcus hadn't signed his death certificate with me. I spent the remainder of my evening packing our things and cleaning the house. I couldn't imagine leaving my home unkempt when I was away. I'd always had this fear about leaving home for the day and never making it back alive. Salene would not only have to make my final arrangements, but clean as well. I chuckled just thinking about how well she knew me. She knew I would haunt her from my grave if there was so much as one fiber out of place throughout my castle. I made sure to grab some extra cash from my emergency stash just in case I lost the ability to maintain my sanity and required money for bail on this "I'm sorry I've been fucking you over" vacation.

After I completed my household chores and everything was all packed up, I wound down to a nice glass of cabernet and some smooth jazz. I enjoyed a nice hot bubble bath and rehearsed a few of my lines for my upcoming argument with Marcus about his infidelity. When I finally found the nerve to confront him, I wanted to be sure not to stumble over any of my words and be able to provide all the facts. I practiced speaking loud and clear and even managed to accomplish it all without any tears or emotion. Although the circumstances weren't ideal, a small part of me was still looking forward to being away from all of my parental and adult responsibilities for a few days. I closed my eyes as I waited for my mind to slow down so I could crash into sleep. I would need as much rest as possible so that I would be bright eyed and bushy tailed when Marcus and I departed for our trip.

The sun was beginning to rise, and I could hear the birds chirping just outside my window. I glanced over at my cell phone and noticed I had a few new messages.

All were from Marcus. One message was from the night before,

Hey little girl, Daddy just wanted to check in on you. Work was a little busy tonight so I will probably be asleep soon, as I am assuming you are as well.

The next messages were from this morning,

Good morning, beautiful, Daddy is just leaving work. I didn't want to call and wake you, because I knew you were probably up late packing and cleaning like the neat freak you are. I need to make a stop at home to grab a few things I will need for our trip. Give Daddy a call when you are awake.

I decided to take a shower and make myself a cup of coffee before returning any of Marcus' calls or messages to clear my mind from the feelings that presented themselves each time we made contact with one another.

Situated comfortably in my favorite robe, I sipped on my freshly brewed cup of Colombian roasted coffee. I decided to give Marcus a call back. The phone rang a few times and there was no answer. Maybe he had fallen asleep. He didn't specify the time we would be leaving for our vacation, but I was sure it would be at some later point of the day. Marcus was always on time for everything. If he didn't make his way straight to me right after work, we definitely had some time to kill.

I sat in solitude while finishing up my coffee. It was nice to finally enjoy a morning without the demands of motherhood or my duties to Marcus. A few more days of this would certainly do me some good. I was actually starting to become more anxious about our upcoming trip. I got so lost in the thought of it all, that I didn't realized how much time had passed. A few hours had gone by and I still had not heard back from him. I was beginning to worry a little. I decided to give Marcus another call just to make sure he was alright. Again, the phone rang and rang with no answer. This was not a part of Marcus' normal behavior to not answer my calls even if he was asleep.

I decided to get dressed and head over to his house to check on him. The distance between our two houses was no more than twenty minutes, but it began to feel like an eternity with each red traffic light and unmoved lane of cars. My heart raced rapidly while worried thoughts consumed me. Had he even made it home after work? What if he was involved in some sort of tragic accident? I drove as fast as I could to get to my love, taking advantage of every shortcut option available. I may have even blown through a few stop signs. I didn't care if a police chase ensued, I needed to find out what had happened. I was just a few minutes away from Marcus' house and still had not received a call back from him. As I parked my vehicle a few feet away from his front door, I noticed his car was parked just outside. A great sigh of relief overcame me. At least I knew he had not been involved in an accident. I headed to the house to check in on him.

Fire Without a Flame

Marcus was quite the sleeper, especially after a long shift. I figured he probably dozed off while packing for our trip. I turned my key quietly and entered. I didn't want to wake him from his rest since I was not sure of the method of travel for our trip. If there was a long drive involved, Marcus would surely need his rest. Once I was inside the house, I could hear the sound of the shower running and music playing loudly from upstairs. A huge sigh of relief ran through my mind. I was happy to find him all in one piece and safe. I noticed his cell phone sitting on the kitchen table. It was no wonder that he did not hear any of my calls. The sound of a ringing phone was no competition for a full music concert and lengthy shower. Though Marcus was on my hit list, I decided what better way to make up from a fight that hadn't taken place yet, than to surprise him by joining him in the shower for a full round of hot and steamy morning sex. I slipped out of my clothes in the kitchen and began to make my way upstairs for a pre-vacation performance.

Just as I made my way to the first step, the curiosity in me realized I had just been presented with another perfect opportunity to take a look into Marcus' cell phone to see if Miss Star and him had been in recent contact. I went back and began to scroll through his messages but was immediately intrigued by the number count on his photo gallery application. What better proof of what the hell was going on between the two of them than evidence that included photos? I mean, a picture is worth a thousand words, right? I began to scroll through the photos. I found mostly what I suspected: many pictures of myself, Dylan, Marcus' son Ryan, and the four of us together at various events over the past year. My heart was warmed. I could feel the trust that I had lost for Marcus since his act of infidelity slowly returning to me. The desire to snoop through Marcus' messages instantly left me. My man really loved me and our little family.

I decided we could talk about what I witnessed at the mall, shed some light on the situation, and work through it. I really loved Marcus a lot, and I believed what we had was definitely worth fighting for. I felt more eager to get upstairs and join him in the shower. Just as I was about to return his phone to where I'd found it, I noticed an unusual icon on his home screen. Marcus and I had the same cellphone model and the majority of our applications were the same. I was not familiar with this icon that I'd discovered. I double tapped on it to satisfy my curiosity. As soon as the app opened up, a slew of photos and videos displayed. Marcus was quite the technological genius. There must have been some sort of additional memory space for his photos that he utilized. I began to scroll the pictures one by one. Immediately my heart stopped and then dropped to the table. There had to have been countless numbers of photos and videos of various women. Tears began to fill my eyes, but somehow the pain required me to continue to browse through the gallery. There were nude photos and homemade pornography videos everywhere! One by one, I opened them up and zoomed in. He had photos of himself and the girl from the mall kissing and posing together. There were even videos of the two having sex. The faster I scrolled, the more tears of pain ran down my cheeks.

There were photos of another woman, but her face was hidden behind a masquerade costume mask. Marcus loved for me to dress up similarly for him when we role played. I guess I was not the only one. This was truly unbelievable. It was time for me to confront this whore of a man that had been obviously playing with my heart for quite some time now. Before I put down the phone, there was one more video that sort of caught my attention to view. I pressed "play" and couldn't believe what I was witnessing. It was a video of that little bitch from the restaurant that Marcus had taken me to on our first date about a year ago. I could never forget her face. Allure was her name. She had been our waitress for the evening. The video showed that bitch performing oral sex on Marcus right at the restaurant. In fact, it appeared to be from the night of our date.

It was all coming back to me now! How could I have been so foolish!? I remember returning from the restroom that evening and seeing Allure quickly returning to an upright position as if she were retrieving something from the floor just beneath Marcus' chair. I should have known the two of them had to have been previously acquainted. I'd seen enough. I put the phone down, replaced every article of my clothing, and then headed for the kitchen to grab a knife. I was going to chop Marcus' body into tiny pieces of memory. A slice for every ounce of pain he had caused me. I couldn't believe he'd been living such a lie this entire time.

As I walked up the stairs, face completely covered in tears and disappointment, I could hear giggling coming from the bathroom. They appeared to be the sounds of a woman. This morning was becoming more and more upsetting by the minute. I approached the bathroom door with the butcher knife in hand. I quietly pushed on the door so that it sat ajar. I peeped through the small crack. Through the thick of the fog that formed from the steam of the running shower and good times being had by Marcus and the whore that accompanied him, I was able to line up my targets. I would stab him first and once he was down for the count, she would be next. The two of them couldn't hear death quickly approaching them because they were so lost in their bath time fun.

My rage could no longer be contained. With every ounce of strength I had in me, I raised my foot just about three inches from the floor and kicked in the bathroom door like a Federal Marshall looking for a fugitive. The music was loud but not enough to muffle my unannounced visit to Marcus and his guest. I could hear the screams of surprise and fear coming from Marcus and who I could now identify as Star from the mall. I began to charge towards them both as I snatched back the shower curtain to put my butcher knife in full viewing pleasure.

"Ava! Ava!" Marcus shouted. "Put down the knife, baby! Please let me explain!"

"I hate you! You cheating bastard!" I shouted while wielding the knife around looking to see whose flesh would get a sample of this sharp blade first. Star backed herself into the furthest corner of the shower walls. The music was still playing loudly, but I didn't care. Maybe the neighbors wouldn't be able to hear the screams of my victims as life left and death entered. Suddenly, Marcus grabbed my wrist and attempted to disarm me. I was so angry that I had developed strength I'd never known before. Marcus and I tussled around competing for the knife. Suddenly a splatter of blood hit the white walls and tiled floors. I couldn't tell if it was mine or his. We continued to wrestle. Star began screaming louder and this time she let out something that became more infuriating to me.

"Allure! Allure! Please come help!"

Fire Without a Flame

I looked over to the bathroom door and in came little Miss Waitress from the restaurant. The shit was something out of a horror movie. It was me and my broken heart against the three of them. It didn't matter to me whether I lived or died in that moment. Dylan would be well provided for under Salene's care.

She was still young enough that she would probably forget we'd ever met in a few years. Someone had to be leaving this house in a body bag, and if it was going to be me I wouldn't be leaving here without a fight. The waitress attempted to come close to me to assist Marcus in retrieving the knife. I began to swing more violently. The small space in the bathroom was filled to capacity. There just wasn't enough room for my enragement and the three little whores.

"Let's just talk about this, Ava!" Marcus pleaded. "Please put down the knife before someone gets hurt really badly."

By now I could tell that it was Marcus whose blood had saturated the floors and walls like a fresh coat of maroon colored paint. He was bleeding from his arm. As much as I was hurting at this moment, I wanted to stop and tend to his wound. I was so conditioned to care for him and meeting all of his needs that even in a moment of extreme dysfunction, I felt obligated to serve him. The two girls just stood there with tears falling from their eyes, their faces displaying undeniable fear. They were both naked and unsure if they would make it out of this bathroom. I couldn't confirm their fate myself. Emotions were running high and I was too numb to care about anyone's feelings. I just wanted to undo all of this. If only I had stayed home and waited for Marcus instead of just showing up here. Or maybe if I hadn't been so thoughtful and attempted to surprise him with a gift, none of this would be happening right now.

"Ava, if you don't calm down and hand me the knife, I could bleed to death and die. You have too much to lose. Please think about Dylan," he said.

"Don't you dare mention my baby's name in front of these whores!" I shouted. "You should have considered Dylan while you were out parading the city without any pants on! You make me sick!" I shouted. "Are there any more of these whores hiding throughout the rest of the house?" I asked.

"Ava, please hand me the knife, and I promise to explain everything." I began to feel the room spinning. My legs became weakened, and I just fell to the floor. Marcus quickly reached for the knife and handed it to the waitress. She and the mall whore embraced one another and quickly ran out of the bathroom. I figured they were running off to go and call the police on me. I really didn't care if that was the case. I rested my head in the palm of my hands as I sat in the pool of Marcus' blood. He grabbed me tight and held me. He kept apologizing for what had unfolded and begged me to stick around to hear him out.

"If you'll just give me a few minutes to clean myself up, I promise I will shed light on the whole situation." I didn't have any strength left in me to put up a fight. Marcus picked me up from off of the floor and escorted me to the spare bedroom. "Please stay here while I get cleaned up and calm the other girls," he said. I could barely open my eyes from all of the crying and anxiety. I was too weak to move so I sat idle, almost in a state of paralysis.

Fire Without a Flame

Some time had gone by and Marcus came back into the room. His arm was fully bandaged, and he was carrying a piece of paper in his hand. He found a seat at a safe distance from me just across the room.

"Ava, there is something I need to tell you," he started.

"No shit, motherfucker!" I replied in anger.

"Hear me out please," he pleaded.

"I'm listening," I said.

"Those two girls are not some random women that I just met," he said. The next thing I expected to hear from this asshole was that they were his sisters or some sick shit. "They are my wives," he finished. As if my heart could take any more pain.

"What the hell do you mean, Marcus?!" I arose from the bed and headed in his direction. I wanted to beat the remainder of life out of him. I didn't care if he had lost quarts of blood in that bathroom, I was coming for more.

"Ava, please allow me to finish," he pleaded.

"You are done here, Marcus! There is nothing left to be said!" I screamed. "You can't possibly be married to multiple women at the same time! It's illegal! When the hell would you have time to marry while we were together?" As if this entire preposterous situation warranted further explanation.

"Ava, the day we met was not a coincidence," he began. "When you stopped into the auto body shop that day, it was all intentional."

"What the hell are you talking about, Marcus?" I asked, now more afraid and confused than I've ever been in my entire life.

185

Geneya Singleton

"When you brought your car to Stan's auto body shop
for the first time to have your air conditioning repaired,
I was there. I spotted you immediately and you caught
my attention. You were so beautiful and unforgettably
kind. You were so comfortable speaking to Stan about
your life and struggles as a single mother. Stan knew that
I had been in search of a playmate for my wives and
myself, and he'd felt you would be the perfect fit. After
hearing so many wonderful things about you as a mother
and a woman, I knew I had to have you. We intentionally
repaired your car improperly because we both knew you
weren't in the mental space to be picked up by some
random guy working at an auto body shop. Because you
were a vulnerable single woman, setting up a plan to have
me appear to be the perfect gentleman and an
exceedingly helpful employee after you had to return to
Stan's shop for the second time for the very same issue
with your car would allow me to gain your trust, and
hence make for an easy transition," he finished.

I felt like I was going to faint at any moment listening
to all of this foolishness unfold. Was I being punked or
something? This was definitely something you would
find on a Sunday afternoon Lifetime movie. I wanted
nothing more than to awaken from this dream.

"So, this was all a game of charades with you,
Marcus?" I asked, as if I really wanted to know the
answer.

"No, Ava! Although initially I had been in search of a
playmate for myself and my wives, as time passed I
developed serious feelings for you," he said. "I love you.
I love Dylan like she was my own daughter. The other
wives have known about you and they agree that you will
make a perfect fit for my third wife. I was going to speak
with you about it during our vacation. I have a copy of

your contract here in my hands. I know you are extremely upset and confused right now and if you need a few days to think it over, I can be patient."

He could not be serious at all right now, I thought. Why was this happening to me? Was this some sort of karmic retribution? I had never done anything wrong to anyone. I lifted my head from the palm of my hands to now find that he was standing closer to me, still holding those stupid ass papers in his hand. He appeared to be really serious about this whole nightmare. The audacity that Marcus had to insult my intelligence. If he thought for one second that I would play any part in this circus act, he had another thing coming. I leaped from the bed and ran toward the stairs. I could hear Marcus calling for me, but it made no sense to turn back and respond to a person and place that I would never see again. I had to get out of this house immediately. I made it to the front door and saw no signs of the waitress or the mall whore, or should I say, Mrs. and Mrs. Marcus? That didn't even sound realistic in my own head. How would it sound to the world and my family and friends?

I finally made it to the other side of this nightmare house and headed straight for my car. No one would believe any of this. Hell, even I didn't, and I was present to witness it all. I was so disappointed in myself for allowing another man to betray me the way Anthony had done. As I reached for the driver side door, I became more infuriated and embarrassed by it all. I couldn't leave without making the message loud and clear that no one would ever fuck over Ava Hampton again in life and live to tell about it. At least not without some sort of scar to go along with their story. I headed for my trunk where I kept a baseball bat for protection.

Geneya Singleton

Good ole Minnie was a 32 inch, aluminum stick of fun and that was exactly what I was about to have, some justified, self-rewarding fun. I began walking in the direction of Marcus' car and swung Minnie as far back as my arms would take her and released. The sound of glass shattering filled the afternoon skies. People walking by began to stop and stare. I had no care left in me. I moved on to the next window and broke it out. Before I knew it, I had made my way around the entire car. There wasn't a window left on it to be shattered. Pounds of broken glass shimmered on the ground against the sun. I could hear people chattering and suddenly, I heard police sirens. I ran to my vehicle as quickly as I could to make a run for it. Tears filled my eyes and blurred my vision, but I made it home.

My heart was broken, and my hands were bleeding everywhere from my enraged destruction. I nervously exited my car after I cleared the coast of any nearby law enforcement. I made a quick dash to my front door. Once inside, I collapsed on the floor. I cried for what seemed like hours. My phone rang continuously with calls from Marcus. I wouldn't dare to answer. Suddenly there was loud knocking at my front door. I kept quiet in hopes that whoever it was would just go away. The knocking turned into much louder banging, and then I could hear the announcement on what sounded like a bullhorn.

"Ava Hampton, this is the local police department. Come out with your hands up, or we will break down the door." I reached for my phone to make a quick call to Salene. If I was going away to prison, she would have to come to care for my Dylan.

"Hey, girl. What's up?" she answered.

"There was blood and glass everywhere," I said. "The police are here now. Please come get my Dylan from Sophie," I finished.

I could hear Salene shouting on the other end of the phone before I disconnected the call. Before I could say another word, I heard a loud noise which sounded like a bomb exploding. They were in the house now. I lay on my stomach and voiced my intentions of total surrender as I came face to face with three or four pairs of black leather boots. The cold from the handcuffs took some of the burn from the open cuts along my wrists and hands. As they read me my rights, all I could do was think about my poor Dylan and if I would ever see her again.

The fire that burned without a flame was now extinguished by pain yet again.

Connect
with the Author

Website: www.firewithoutaflame.com

Facebook: @firewithoutaflame_

Instagram: @firewithoutaflame_

Twitter: @firewithoutafl1

Email: authorgeneyasingleton@gmail.com

Creative Control With Self-Publishing

Divine Legacy Publishing provides authors with the guid-ance necessary to take creative control of their work through self-publishing. We provide:

Writing Coaching

Professional Editing

Author Branding

Self-Publishing Coaching

Graphic Design

Website Design

Let Divine Legacy Publishing help you master the business of self-publishing.

Made in the USA
Middletown, DE
09 November 2023

42285939R00118